Goodbye,
Sweet Prince

Christy® Fiction Series

Christy® Fiction Series

Goodbye, Sweet Prince

Catherine Marshall

adapted by C. Archer

Thomas Nelson, Inc.

Nashville

GOODBYE, SWEET PRINCE
Book Eleven in the *Christy*® Fiction Series

Copyright © 1997
by Marshall-LeSourd L.L.C.

The *Christy*® Fiction Series is based on *Christy*®
by Catherine Marshall © 1967.

The *Christy*® name and logo are officially registered
trademarks of Marshall-LeSourd L.L.C.

Managing Editor: Laura Minchew
Project Editor: Beverly Phillips

Scripture quotations are from the
King James Version of the Bible.

Library of Congress Cataloging-in-Publication Data

Archer, C. 1956–
    Goodbye, sweet Prince / Catherine Marshall ; adapted by C. Archer.
        p.   cm. — (Christy fiction series ; 11)
    Summary: When the mountain mission where she teaches must
sell its beautiful black stallion, a heartbroken Christy watches as
Prince is auctioned to the highest bidder.
    ISBN 0–8499–3962–3 (pbk.)
    [1. Teachers—Fiction. 2. Mountain life—Fiction. 3. Christian
life—Fiction. 4. Horses—Fiction.] I. Marshall, Catherine, 1914–
1983. II. Title. III. Series : Archer, C., 1956–   Christy fiction
series ; 11.
PZ7.A6744Go   1997
[Fic]—dc21

                                                    97–532
                                                    CIP
                                                    AC

Printed in the United States of America

97 98 99 00 01 02 OPM 9 8 7 6 5 4 3 2 1

The Characters

CHRISTY RUDD HUDDLESTON, a nineteen-year-old girl.

CHRISTY'S STUDENTS:
- CREED ALLEN, age nine.
- LITTLE BURL ALLEN, age six.
- DELLA MAY ALLEN, age eight.
- ROB ALLEN, age fourteen.
- WANDA BECK, age eight.
- BESSIE COBURN, age twelve.
- WRAIGHT HOLT, age seventeen.
- RUBY MAE MORRISON, age thirteen.
- MOUNTIE O'TEALE, age ten.
- CLARA SPENCER, age twelve.
- LUNDY TAYLOR, age seventeen.
- HANNAH WASHINGTON, age eight.

DAVID GRANTLAND, the young minister.

IDA GRANTLAND, David's sister, and mission housekeeper.

ALICE HENDERSON, a Quaker missionary who started the mission at Cutter Gap.

DR. NEIL MACNEILL, the physician of the Cove.

BEN PENTLAND, the mailman for the Cove.

BIRD'S-EYE TAYLOR, the father of Christy's student Lundy.

MRS. TATUM, a woman who runs a boarding house in El Pano.

JARED COLLINS, the owner of Great Oak Farm.

URIAH WYNNE, an employee on Great Oak Farm.

HANK DREW, the mailman for the area that includes Great Oak Farm.

KETTIE WELLER, a mother of twins.

SHERIFF BELL, the local sheriff.

PRINCE, a black stallion.

OLD THEO, a mule owned by the mission.

GOLDIE, Miss Alice's mare.

❧ One ❧

Happy birthday!"

"Look how big he's grown!"

"I can't wait for him to open his presents!"

Christy Huddleston's students crowded around the birthday boy, applauding and singing.

He stared at them, blinked, then let out a loud snort.

Christy laughed. For a horse, it was a perfectly polite response. "I think Prince wonders what the fuss is all about," she said.

Christy was sitting on the rail fence that enclosed the black stallion's pasture. Her entire class—all seventy students—had gathered there to celebrate Prince's birthday.

The class was supposed to be studying geography this afternoon. But Christy had decided that the children deserved this special treat. Lately, Cutter Gap had fallen on particularly hard times. It was nice to have a reason to celebrate *something*—even if it was just the birthday of a horse.

Of course, Prince wasn't just *any* horse. The magnificent stallion had somehow managed to cast a magic spell over her students. The shy ones grew braver around Prince. The clumsy ones grew confident as they trotted around the pasture on his broad back. And the troublemakers actually seemed to grow calmer. Even Lundy Taylor, the worst bully in the school, acted like a different person around Prince.

Ruby Mae Morrison stepped forward and cleared her throat. "It's time for the present-givin'," she announced.

Quickly, the children fell silent. They'd been planning this for weeks. Ruby Mae, who was thirteen, had been chosen to present Prince's gifts. Although he belonged to the mission, it was Ruby Mae, more than anyone else, who cared for Prince. With the help of the mission minister, David Grantland, she fed Prince, groomed him, and exercised him every day. She was also the most accomplished rider of all the children.

"Before we start," Ruby Mae announced, "I have to tell the truth. We don't rightly know for sure and certain that today is Prince's birthday." Gently, she scratched the stallion's nose. "Since he was a present to the mission, nobody exactly knows when he was born, 'ceptin' that he's about three years old. But I took a vote, and we figured today would be a fine day to have a birthday."

Bessie Coburn, one of Ruby Mae's best friends, elbowed Ruby Mae in the ribs. "The presents, Ruby Mae! Get to the presents!"

"All right, then. First off, the necklace!"

Hannah Washington and Della May Allen paraded over solemnly, carrying a large round garland. It was made of woven twigs, flowers, and berries. Carefully, they placed it around Prince's glossy neck.

"He's eatin' the berries!" Hannah exclaimed. "He likes it!"

Everyone laughed. It was a nice moment, one that Christy had feared she would never see when Hannah's family, the descendants of slaves, had first come to this isolated mountain cove. Her dark skin had set her apart, and it had broken Christy's heart to see the ignorance and prejudice Hannah and her family had endured.

But Hannah had persevered, and Prince had done his part to help her. Like Ruby Mae, Hannah was a gifted rider. By offering to teach several of the children what she knew about riding, she'd found a way to reach them and to make some real friends.

"And now," Ruby Mae continued, "for the next present!"

Mountie O'Teale stepped up to Prince's

side. She was a small girl for her ten years, shy and self-conscious around strangers because of a lingering speech problem. Still, whenever Mountie was around Prince, she blossomed. Her speech flowed, and her smiles came quickly.

"This is for you, Prince," Mountie announced in a clear voice, rich with the mountain accent Christy never tired of hearing. "It's for keepin' you warm on winter nights. And we all put in a bit of it."

Mountie held out the precious gift—a horse blanket sewn together like a patchwork quilt. With Ruby Mae's help, she placed the blanket over Prince's back.

As Mountie adjusted the blanket, Christy's eyes filled with tears. A square of fabric was missing from the sleeve of Mountie's worn, tattered dress. The other children had similar missing patches, since they'd each donated a piece of fabric for the quilt.

"It's beautiful, children," Christy said softly. "Prince is a very lucky fellow."

The blanket had been the children's idea. Christy had resisted the notion at first, knowing how little they could afford to sacrifice— even a square inch of clothing. As it was, most of the children were shoeless year-round, and they all wore hand-me-downs or donations from churches. To cut into those precious clothes for a horse's birthday present?

As much as Christy understood their desire to give, she just didn't think it was a sacrifice they could afford to make.

But one evening, Miss Alice Henderson, the woman who had helped found the mission, had taken Christy aside. "'It is more blessed to give than to receive,'" she'd told Christy. "Perhaps this is a sacrifice the children would like to make."

"But now?" Christy had asked. "The mission's never been so short on donations and cash. We've been scraping by for weeks, living on hope and prayers. The last thing the children need is to be giving away the clothes off their own backs. For a horse's birthday, no less!"

"Maybe," Miss Alice had replied, "that's exactly why they need it. Maybe Prince's birthday provides them with a reason to celebrate. We all need to be able to give, Christy."

Out had come the scissors. One by one, Christy had cut tiny squares out of her students' precious clothes.

"It's just like Joseph's coat o' many colors!" Ruby Mae exclaimed. "Ain't it just the purtiest thing you ever did see?"

As if on command, Prince sauntered around in a circle, showing off his new blanket and garland. With his head held high and his mane streaming in the wind, he was a wonderful sight.

"Would you look at that?" David called as he strode toward the fence. "Children, that is, without a doubt, the finest horse blanket in the history of horse blankets! And look how Prince is dancing about! I can tell he loves it. Judging from the way he's trying to eat his garland, he seems to love that, too!"

Prince trotted around while the children followed him, laughing and joking. "I haven't seen them in such a good mood in a long time," Christy whispered to David. "It's good to see. They love that horse so much."

A frown creased David's brow. He glanced back at the mission house.

"David?" Christy asked. "What's wrong?"

"I . . ." He paused. "The truth is, Christy, I'm not sure how much longer we're going to be able to keep Prince."

⫷ TWO ⫸

Miss Ida," Christy said at dinner that evening, "that was a very nice soup. What do you call it?"

"Whatever Soup," said Miss Ida, who was David's sister. "I toss whatever I can find into the pot and let it boil. Tonight it was potatoes, some roots Ruby Mae dug up, and half an onion."

"Well, at least we're not resorting to boiling shoe leather," David joked.

"Don't be too sure, David." Miss Ida started to clear the table. "Remember how tough that meat was last night?"

David gulped as Miss Ida headed to the kitchen. "She *was* joking, wasn't she?"

"Preacher, 'course she was *jokin'*." Ruby Mae rolled her eyes. "Shoe leather's way too precious to waste on eatin'."

Miss Alice sighed. "The sad truth is, we are going to have to do some belt-tightening." She motioned toward the kitchen. "Ruby Mae, you go on and help Miss Ida clean up. Christy and David and I have some things to discuss."

"Uh-oh." Ruby Mae leapt out of her chair. "I hate discussions. There's always a heap o' loud voices. Leastways, that's how it always was with my ma and step-pa."

She grabbed her plate and mug, tossed her head, and dashed for the kitchen, her long, red hair flying like a flag in the breeze. Because Ruby Mae had a hard time getting along with her stepfather, she was living at the mission house for the time being. She could be a handful sometimes, but everyone was very fond of her.

Miss Alice led David and Christy to the parlor. She pointed to a wooden box. "Take a look," she said. "That's the latest round of donations."

Christy peeked inside. The half-empty box contained a few threadbare clothes and some musty books.

"We have to face facts," Miss Alice said. "The mission is very low on funds. We're short on food and supplies, and most importantly, on medicine."

Christy couldn't help feeling alarmed at her tone. Miss Alice was always calm in a crisis.

No matter what the problem was, she always seemed to have a solution. But today, she looked genuinely worried. Her gray eyes were rimmed in red, and the smile lines around her eyes looked more like deep worry lines.

"The mission's always struggling to make ends meet, Miss Alice," Christy pointed out. "Perhaps if I send some more letters, asking for donations—"

"This is far more serious than that, Christy." Miss Alice rubbed her eyes. "Doctor MacNeill and I are dreadfully short on medical supplies. Miss Ida is running out of food. I'm afraid this is going to call for some drastic actions."

Christy didn't know what to say. She walked to the window, trying to collect her thoughts. The deep green spires of the Great Smoky Mountains loomed in the distance. Once again, she was struck by the contrasts in this wondrous landscape. How could a land so rich in beauty be inhabited by people so desperately poor?

"I think," Miss Alice said softly, "that we only have one choice. We need to sell something of value. And the most valuable thing the mission owns is Prince."

David nodded gravely. He looked sadder than Christy had ever seen him. Christy knew he loved that horse as much as the children did.

"You're right, Miss Alice," he said softly. "There's an auction in El Pano next week. I'll take him myself."

"I'm so sorry, David. If I could think of another way . . ." Miss Alice's voice trailed off. "Old Theo wouldn't bring us much. As lame as he is, we'd have to pay somebody to take that poor old mule off our hands. And Goldie's a fine mare, but she's getting up there in years. If we didn't get enough for her, we'd have to sell Prince later on, too. And we can't afford to lose both horses. It's the only way we can get to the most remote parts of these mountains."

"But the children will be heartbroken," Christy protested. "There must be another way. Maybe if I went home to Asheville, I could ask for donations from churches. Or I could even get a job for a while. . . ."

"And how would that help the children?" Miss Alice asked. "They need you here, Christy. No, I'm afraid this is the only way."

Christy dropped into a chair next to David. For a while, nobody spoke.

Finally, Christy broke the silence. "Remember when Mr. Pentland delivered Prince to us at the school?" she asked with a wistful smile. "I can still hear him calling out 'Special delivery from the U-nited States Postal Service!' Who would ever have imagined the mailman was delivering a huge black stallion? The

10

children were so thrilled I thought I'd never get them to settle down again!"

"It was a very generous donation," Miss Alice agreed. A woman who had met Christy's mother in Asheville, North Carolina, had sent Prince after learning of the mission's need for a horse. "And we've been blessed to have such a fine animal as a companion. But I'm sure David will find him a fine new home. Perhaps, if it's close enough, we could even take the children to visit sometimes."

Just then, Ruby Mae appeared in the doorway. "Visit who?"

"Ruby Mae," Christy said, "you know you shouldn't eavesdrop!"

"I weren't eavesdroppin'. Miss Ida done sent me to see if'n anybody wants some tea. She's got some herbs she's been savin'." She planted her hands on her hips. "So who would we be a-visitin'? The doctor's Aunt Cora in Knoxville, maybe? Or Miz Christy's folks back in Asheville?"

"No, Ruby Mae." Miss Alice cast a quick glance at Christy. "I'm afraid we've got some bad news, dear."

"What kind of bad news?"

"The mission needs money, Ruby Mae," Christy said gently. "Very, very badly. Now, you know how much we all love Prince, but—"

"Prince?" Ruby Mae asked. "What does

11

Prince have to do with it?" Suddenly, her eyes went wide. "Unless . . . unless you all are a-plannin' to sell him?"

"It's the only way," David said. "You know I love that horse as much as you do, Ruby Mae. You know I'd do anything to try to keep him if I could."

"You don't love him like I do!" Ruby Mae shouted. "Nobody does! You ain't the one who knows just where he likes to be scratched behind his right ear! You ain't the one who's kissed him goodnight ever' single evenin' since he come to Cutter Gap!" A sob racked her body. "Nobody loves him like I love him! You can't sell him! You just can't!"

"There isn't any choice, Ruby Mae," Christy said. She tried to embrace her, but Ruby Mae yanked free.

"I'll never forgive you for this," Ruby Mae sobbed. "Never, not as long as I live!"

She spun around and ran up the stairs. In the silence that followed, her awful sobs seemed to fill the whole house.

✺ Three ✺

I suppose most of you know that tomorrow the Reverend Grantland and Ruby Mae and I will be taking Prince to the auction in El Pano," Christy said the following Thursday morning at school. "Miss Alice will be teaching you tomorrow. I expect you all to be on your best behavior."

A few days had passed. By now, everybody knew about the decision to sell Prince. All week, Christy had dealt with the pleading and tears of her students.

Wraight Holt had threatened to kidnap Prince and hide him in a safe area no one could find. (Fortunately, Christy had talked him out of that scheme.) Creed Allen had offered to sell his new litter of hound dogs in exchange for Prince's safety. Everybody, it seemed, had a plan for saving Prince.

But in the end, there was nothing anyone could do. Standing before her class today, Christy realized that this was the hardest lesson she'd had to teach her students. How could she help the children accept a loss like this . . . children who had so little to lose and who'd suffered through so much?

She patted Clara Spencer on the shoulder. Like so many of the students, Clara's eyes were red, and she was sniffling softly.

"I know how hard this is," Christy said as she walked past the rows of desks and benches. "But loss is a part of life, children. With God's help, we'll make it through this sad time. Who knows what the future may bring? Maybe someday we'll read about Prince after he's become a famous racehorse. Can anybody else think of another happy ending to this story?"

After a moment, Creed raised his hand. "Maybe he'll grow up to be a daddy and have lots of little Princes runnin' around."

"That's a wonderful idea, Creed. Anybody else?"

"He could go to a farm where they grow lots and lots of sugar, 'cause he loves sugar more 'n anything," Little Burl Allen suggested. "And he could get fat and sassy like my ol' hound dog."

"That would be a very happy future for Prince," Christy agreed.

Ruby Mae glared at Christy. "Them's just fairy tales. Ain't but one good future for Prince," she said. "That's when we find a way to keep him here in Cutter Gap, where he belongs."

The answer didn't surprise Christy. Since she'd found out they'd have to sell Prince, Ruby Mae had barely spoken to Christy. Each evening at dinner, she simply stared at her plate. In school, she refused to answer questions. She'd spent every spare moment she could find with Prince.

"That's such a nice dream, Ruby Mae," Christy said gently. "But I think we have to accept the fact that Prince won't be living here anymore."

"I ain't never goin' to accept that," Ruby Mae muttered. Someone else sobbed. Another student sniffled.

Christy couldn't help sighing. She wanted to cry herself. She'd be very glad when this whole thing was over. With time, the children's pain would ease.

At least, that's what she hoped.

—◆ ◆ ◆—

"You're sure you want to come?" David asked the next morning. "It's a long, hard walk to El Pano. And I'm sure you remember how tough the trail can be, Christy."

15

"Don't try to talk me out of it, David," Christy answered. "I'm coming."

"I'm comin', too, no matter what you say," Ruby Mae agreed. "I got to say goodbye, proper-like."

It was a cool, breezy day. Wisps of clouds flew past the mountaintops like ships on a pale blue ocean. In the pasture, Prince was grazing calmly.

"Look how happy Prince is. He don't even know what's a-comin'," Ruby Mae said. "He thinks he can trust us."

"I know you think we're betraying Prince, Ruby Mae," David said as he leaned against the fence. "But we're going to make sure he gets a good home. I promise."

Ruby Mae jutted her chin. "S'posin' *your* ma and pa sold you? How do you think that'd make you feel?"

"It's not like that, Ruby Mae," Christy said. But even as she said the words, she realized that for Ruby Mae, this goodbye was probably especially hard. Perhaps she felt a little abandoned herself, living with Christy and Miss Ida at the mission house. Ruby Mae hardly ever saw her mother or her stepfather. Watching Prince being torn from his "family" couldn't be easy. Still, she did at least seem somewhat more resigned to the fact that he was leaving.

Off in the distance came the sound of a

galloping horse. "Looks like Doctor MacNeill," Ruby Mae reported. "And there's someone ridin' with him."

"That's Lundy Taylor!" Christy exclaimed.

Doctor MacNeill reined his horse to a stop, and he and Lundy dismounted. "Thought I'd stop by to wish you a safe trip," the doctor said, winking at Christy.

David pretended to bat his eyes. "Why, Neil, I didn't know you cared!"

The doctor laughed. "Actually, I was talking to Christy, Reverend."

"Now, there's a surprise," David said. David and Neil had been rivals for Christy's affections for some time.

"In any case, it was nice of you to come, Neil," Christy said. "And what brings you here, Lundy?"

Lundy shrugged. "Doc and me crossed paths up yonder on the ridge. Said he'd give me a ride."

"Lundy has something he wants to give to Prince," the doctor explained. He pointed to the burlap sack Lundy had hoisted over his shoulder.

Lundy grimaced. He was a dark, hulking young man with a threatening swagger. Christy had always been a little bit afraid of him, although she tried not to show it. But today, strangely enough, Lundy seemed almost shy.

17

"Ain't nothin' much," Lundy said.

"Figures," muttered Ruby Mae. Like most of Christy's students, she wasn't exactly fond of the bully.

"Well, we'd better call Prince over here," David said. "You know how he loves gifts."

He let out a shrill whistle. Instantly, Prince swung around and trotted over to the fence. Lundy reached up and scratched the stallion's nose. "Hey, ol' Prince. Looky here. I brung you somethin'. On account o' your goin' away and all."

Ruby Mae looked a little annoyed. "We already done all the presents at his birthday party, Lundy."

"This is different," Lundy said, his eyes locked on Prince. "This is . . . special. He ain't just yours, Ruby Mae Morrison."

Lundy reached into the burlap sack and pulled out a simple, homely bridle. He held it out and Prince sniffed at it happily.

"I made it outa some deer hide I was a-savin'. Pa said I was a fool to waste it." Lundy hesitated. "Whopped me good over it, truth to tell."

Christy winced. Lundy's father, Bird's-Eye, had a notorious bad temper.

"It's beautiful, Lundy," she said.

"No, it ain't," Lundy replied matter-of-factly. "I ain't much for makin' things. But the leather's soft as it comes. It'll feel nice on his face. And see? I cut his name into the leather."

He held up the bridle. Sure enough, he'd crudely carved letters into the leather:

PRINS

Christy saw Ruby Mae open her mouth to speak. She knew what was coming next— some nasty comment about the bridle, or the fact that Lundy did so poorly in school. Goodness knew that Lundy deserved the wrath of his fellow students, as much as he'd bullied them all. Still, Christy couldn't help cringing as she waited for the hurtful remark.

"It's . . ." Ruby Mae's gaze darted from Lundy to Prince and back again. Lundy touched the stallion's nose, his eyes filled with tears.

Ruby Mae took a deep breath. "It's a wondrous bridle, Lundy," she said softly. "Prince'll be mighty proud to wear it, I reckon."

"Thanks, Ruby Mae," Lundy whispered.

Ruby Mae hopped over the fence and gestured for Lundy to follow. "Come on. I'll help you put it on him. He'll be the finest horse for sure at the auction." She shook her head. "Much as it hurts me to say so."

❧ Four ❧

It's such a shame, havin' to sell that fine animal. But I'm sure you'll get yourselves a fair price," said Mrs. Tatum, the owner of the boarding house in El Pano.

It was Saturday morning. Christy, Ruby Mae, and David had spent the night in Mrs. Tatum's Victorian frame house. It was the same place Christy had stayed when she had first come to Tennessee some months ago.

"I want to thank you again for taking us in, Mrs. Tatum," David said, "and I promise you that as soon as we sell Prince, we'll pay you for our rooms."

"Nonsense," said the tall, big-boned woman. "I wouldn't hear of it. Me, take money from a man of the cloth and a fine teacher like Miss Huddleston? Not likely." She slipped a basket over Ruby Mae's arm. "Now, there's plenty of my famous spareribs and pickled beans in here to keep you goin'."

"Mrs. Tatum, you're too kind," Christy said.

"I'm just glad to see you've survived in Cutter Gap." Mrs. Tatum smiled at David. "To tell you the truth, I didn't think this mite of a gal, all of nineteen years, would last a week in that out-of-the-way place. It's a miracle, I tell you."

"Christy's tougher than she looks, believe me," David said fondly.

"Well, I guess you'd best be gettin' on. The auction barn's about a quarter mile down yonder. You can't miss it. There'll be folks comin' from miles around. Most of them are just there to watch, not to buy. There's maybe half a dozen big spenders. And 'course, there's Mr. Jared Collins."

"Who's he?" Ruby Mae asked.

"Just the richest man in these here parts. Owns Great Oak Farm, and makes most of his money buyin' and sellin' horses. He's quite the fancy gentleman. You can't miss him. Just look for the golden riding crop. He carries it everywhere with him."

David and Christy set off toward the auction barn, with Ruby Mae astride Prince. Mrs. Tatum had been right. The barn was easy to find. A steady stream of people were heading in that direction.

"You know," Ruby Mae said, "I was just thinkin'. This'll be the last time I ride Prince, forever and ever." She cast a desperate look at David. "Preacher, you sure there ain't some other way?"

"I'm sure, Ruby Mae."

She gave a resigned nod and said nothing more until they reached the auction site.

The auction barn was bustling with activity. It smelled of hay and leather and horse. The center was ringed off, and around the ring were bleachers where observers and bidders could watch the horses come and go. Most of the people there looked like simple farmers, dressed in plain clothes or overalls. But a few, as Mrs. Tatum had predicted, looked very well-to-do.

David went to talk to one of the auctioneers. He returned a few minutes later. "We're supposed to take Prince to stall number one," he explained. "The bidders will come by to take a look at him before the actual auction takes place."

"Then what?" Ruby Mae asked.

"Then we wait for his number to be called, and they'll lead him into the center ring for the bidding. Since he's number one, he'll probably be the first horse out."

The stalls were located on the far side of the barn. Ruby Mae led Prince into the stall marked "one." Next door, a young boy was busily brushing the mane of a dapple gray mare.

When he saw Prince, he let out a low

whistle. "Whoa. He's bound to fetch a pretty penny," he said.

Ruby Mae didn't answer. The boy held out his brush. "Want to clean him up? He'll get a better bid if'n he's lookin' shiny."

"Prince don't need no brush," Ruby Mae said. "He's already plenty beautiful."

"Suit yourself."

Down the aisle came prospective buyers, one by one. All of them, it seemed, stopped to admire Prince.

The first was a tall man with small, black eyes. He was accompanied by a shorter, grizzled-looking companion.

"My name's Lyle Duster," the tall man said. "This here's my brother Ed." Ed coughed softly and stared at the ground. Lyle eyed Prince appreciatively.

"Nice piece o' horseflesh," he muttered.

"Mr. Duster, Prince ain't no horseflesh," Ruby Mae replied angrily. "He's a fine animal who just happens to be my friend."

Mr. Duster ignored her.

"An animal like that would do for all our farm work. He's plenty strong to do all the plowin' and run races on weekends, as well."

Ed nodded mutely. David cleared his throat. "I'm sorry, gentlemen, but Prince is only for sale to an owner who won't overwork him. We love him too much to let him work seven days a week."

Lyle Duster spat rudely. "I reckon there's other ways o' gettin' what we want." Ed laughed softly as they walked away.

"Them people give me the willies," Ruby Mae half-whispered to Christy. "Do you reckon they could be thinkin' of stealin' Prince?"

"I certainly hope not," Christy replied. "It sounds as if those people shouldn't own a horse."

A young couple dressed in Sunday finery stopped next. "Clean gaits?" the man asked as he knelt to examine Prince's legs.

"Oh, he's a dream to ride," David replied.

"If'n you don't mind usin' a pillow with your saddle," Ruby Mae muttered under her breath.

"Ruby Mae," Christy scolded when the couple was out of hearing, "there's no point in saying unkind things about Prince. One way or another, he's going to be sold today."

"I know. It's just I hate the way they come and go, pokin' and proddin' like he's a piece o' fruit for sale. He's a livin' creature, Miz Christy. He's got feelings."

"Well, how do you think he feels, hearing you say those things about him?"

"Oh, he don't mind. He knows I'm on his side."

A few minutes later, a tall man with slicked-back hair and a dark mustache paused in front of Prince's stall. He sported a black riding coat and a satin top hat, and in his hand was a riding crop topped with a gold handle.

"Miz Tatum told us about you," Ruby Mae said. "You're the man with all the horses."

"Jared Collins, at your service," the man said, removing his hat and bowing low.

"Are you rich?" Ruby Mae asked.

"Rich? Ah, well, that's all relative, isn't it, my dear? Blessed, perhaps. It's true I do own a few horses. None, I must say, as fine a specimen as this. May I enter the stall?"

Ruby Mae looked surprised. Until then, no one had even bothered to ask her permission. "I s'pose. But watch yourself. He's mighty prickly 'round strangers."

"And who wouldn't be?" the man said in a soft, cooing voice as he stepped into the stall. "All this excitement. All these strangers poring over him like a piece of meat."

Mr. Collins reached into his pocket and pulled out three lumps of sugar. Prince gobbled them up hungrily.

"A sweet tooth, like myself," Mr. Collins said. He smiled at Ruby Mae. "I can tell this horse has been very well cared for. Are you the party responsible?"

"Well, me and the preacher," Ruby Mae replied.

"David Grantland." David shook the man's hand. "And this is Miss Christy Huddleston."

"A pleasure." Mr. Collins took another bow, then turned to scratch Prince's ear.

"Why, that's just how Prince likes it," Ruby Mae observed.

"He's a fine stallion. Anyone would be proud to own him."

"Do you have a nice place for runnin'?" Ruby Mae asked. "Prince loves to run."

"The finest. And the finest food, and the finest trainers . . . and of course, sugar every day." He paused. "Forgive me if I carry on. It's just that to me, these animals are more than something I own. They're a responsibility—a gift."

"You're goin' to bid on him, then?" Ruby Mae asked.

"It would be an honor."

"And s'posin' . . ." Ruby Mae faltered, "s'posin' you bought him. Would you reckon maybe some o' his old friends could stop by for a visit, now and then?"

"Anytime," Mr. Collins responded.

"You a good rider?"

"At the risk of sounding immodest," Mr. Collins said, "I am the finest equestrian in this part of Tennessee."

"That's mighty fine, but what about *ridin'*?" Ruby Mae demanded. "Me, I can ride Prince bareback over a four-foot fence."

Mr. Collins raised a brow. "Such an imaginative girl. How delightful. Now, if you'll excuse me, I must take a look at the other animals here. Although I'm sure there'll be no comparison to . . . what did you say his name was?"

"Prince," Ruby Mae replied.

"A fitting name."

Ruby Mae watched Mr. Collins stride away. "Prince," she said, "I hate to see you go, boy. But if you have to go, I reckon there's worse places to end up."

❧ Five ❧

There he is!" Ruby Mae whispered, squeezing Christy's arm. "It's Prince."

Christy watched as a stable hand led the great stallion into the hay-strewn ring. Prince jerked on his lead rope, then reared up onto his hind legs.

"A spirited one, this horse is!" cried the auctioneer, a heavy-set man with a thick white mustache. "A fine start to the auction indeed!"

The crowd murmured appreciatively as Prince circled the ring.

"He's afeared somethin' terrible," Ruby Mae said. "You can see it in his eyes."

"Ruby Mae, maybe we should wait outside," Christy suggested. "It might be easier—"

"You can git if'n you want," Ruby Mae said. "But I want to see who Prince's new owner's a-goin' to be. I owe him that much, I figure."

"It looks like Mr. Collins is planning to bid," David said. "He's sitting down there in the front row. See?"

"I sure do hope so," Ruby Mae said. "At least then we'd be sure Prince would have a good home. You could tell Mr. Collins loves horses. Almost as much as me, I reckon." She stood, craning her neck to get a better view. "What's goin' to happen now, Preacher?"

"From what I understand, the auctioneer will start the bidding soon. This isn't a big, formal livestock auction like the one I've heard they have in Knoxville. The people who are interested in buying an animal just raise their hands and shout their bids."

"We have here a fine Thoroughbred three-year-old," the auctioneer called out in a rasping voice. "He's owned by the mission over in Cutter Gap."

Prince tossed his head defiantly.

"Feisty," the auctioneer added, "but well-trained."

Ruby Mae nudged David. "Thanks to you and me," she said proudly.

"What do I hear for an opening bid?"

Several hands shot up, and instantly wild shouting began. The bids flew back and forth so quickly that Christy couldn't keep track of them.

"I can't understand the auction-man," Ruby Mae complained. "He's cacklin' faster 'n a mad hen."

"Mr. Collins just made another bid," David said.

Ruby Mae squeezed her eyes shut and clasped her hands together tightly. "Dear God, please let it be Mr. Collins who wins," she prayed aloud, "so that Prince can have all the sugar he ever wants forever and ever. Amen."

She opened one eye. "Was that all right for a prayer, Preacher?"

Just then, the auctioneer cried, "Sold! To Mr. Jared Collins of Great Oak Farm. Congratulations, Mr. Collins, on a fine purchase."

David gave Ruby Mae a hug. "It appears it was an acceptable prayer, Ruby Mae."

"You got what you wanted," Christy said. "Feel a little better?"

"This ain't what I want at all," Ruby Mae replied in a soft voice. "But even if I ain't happy, at least maybe Prince can be."

﹊ ﹊ ﹊

When the sale was over, Christy and Ruby Mae decided to go back to the stalls to say farewell to Prince.

"I'll go on ahead to the cashier and collect the money from Prince's sale," David said.

"Let's meet each other outside the main barn."

"Sure you don't want to come?" Christy asked.

"I've already said my goodbyes. It'll hurt too much to do it again," David murmured.

"We'll just be a few minutes," Christy promised.

"The preacher loves that horse more'n I reckoned," Ruby Mae said as she and Christy made their way through the crowd.

"Yes, he really does."

"I figured . . . I mean, since he was so set on sellin' Prince and all. . . . Well, I guess I figured he didn't care 'bout him like some of us do."

"David loves that horse as much as you do, Ruby Mae. He's just trying to do what's right for the mission."

Prince was stomping around in his stall, tossing his head anxiously. When he caught sight of Ruby Mae, he whinnied softly.

Without another word, Ruby Mae hurried to Prince's stall. Instantly the big horse calmed.

"It's goin' to be all right, boy," she soothed. "You're goin' to be livin' in the finest place around. With all the sugar you can eat."

"This 'un was yours?" asked a gruff older man carrying a new leather bridle.

"Yes," Christy answered. "His name is Prince."

"I'm Uriah Wynne." He gave a terse nod. "Seein' as you know him, maybe you can get this bridle on him. Swear he nearly bit my head off when I tried."

"He's just nervous," Ruby Mae said. "Wouldn't you be, with all these new folks and funny smells?"

"Here." The man thrust the bridle into Ruby Mae's hand. "I'd be much obliged."

"But Prince has already got himself a homemade bridle," Ruby Mae objected.

The man spit on the ground. "I'm just doin' what Mr. C said. Gimme a hand, huh?"

Speaking in low tones to Prince, Ruby Mae quickly removed Lundy's bridle. She handed it to Christy, then dutifully put on the new one. She was just finishing when Mr. Collins strode up.

"Cost me more than I bargained for, but he'll be worth it," he said, "once we get him under control. He's a handful, all right."

"He's awful upset," Ruby Mae said. "Sometimes when he gets like this, it helps if'n you sing 'Amazing Grace' to him. And he loves his new blanket." She pointed to the corner where she'd left the neatly folded blanket. "Me and all my classmates at school, we made it."

"It's certainly . . . colorful. I'll be sure to keep your advice in mind," Mr. Collins said, with a cool smile.

"Mr. Collins, I know this is a great imposition," Christy said, "but one of my students made this bridle for Prince. It would really mean a lot to me if you could take it with him."

"Of course. I'll hang it near his stall, right next to his brass nameplate."

"Thank you so much." Christy turned to Ruby Mae. "Well, I guess it's time to go. We can't delay this forever."

"I know." Ruby Mae rubbed her cheek against Prince's mane. She whispered something to him that no one else could hear. Then, her head held high, she opened the stall door. "Take good care of him," she said, her voice choked.

Christy touched the stallion's nose. "Goodbye, sweet Prince. We'll miss you, boy."

With a nod to Mr. Collins, she put her hand on Ruby Mae's shoulder, and together they started down the aisle.

"Know what I whispered to him?" Ruby Mae said.

"You don't have to tell me," Christy said. "Not if you don't want to."

"I told him someday, somehow, I'd get him back."

Christy wiped away a tear. There was no point in arguing with Ruby Mae. Let her have her tattered hope. They both knew Prince was gone from their lives forever.

As they left the barn, Christy glanced back over her shoulder. Prince was being led away. Mr. Collins was following behind. He paused to toss something into a crate filled with trash, then continued on, basking in the admiring comments from the crowd.

It took Christy a moment before she realized what he'd thrown away.

"Ruby Mae, there's something I want to check. You run on ahead, all right? There's David, over by the cashier. I'll be there in a moment."

Ruby Mae nodded glumly, lost in her own sadness. "Hurry, though, won't you, Miz Christy? I just want to go home now."

Christy ran down the aisle to the pile of trash. Lundy's bridle lay on top. Next to it was Prince's blanket.

She pulled them from the trash. Carefully, she wrapped her shawl around them and tucked the bundle under her arm. Hopefully, Ruby Mae wouldn't ask any questions.

Christy started to call for Mr. Collins, but he had already vanished from view. Maybe, she thought angrily, it was just as well. There was nothing she could say. Prince was his now, and that was that.

❧ Six ❧

I have a special project for all of you today," Christy announced one gloomy afternoon at school.

A week had passed since Prince's sale—a week of tears, moping, pouting, anger, and resignation. Christy had never seen her class so dejected. Finally, she'd decided it was time to take action.

"We're going to write a letter," Christy said, leaning against her battered old desk. "A real, live letter that we're going to mail this afternoon when Mr. Pentland comes."

"Who we goin' to send it to, Teacher?" asked Little Burl Allen.

"Well, I'll give you some hints." Christy closed the window near her desk. A steady, cold rain had sent a damp chill through the schoolhouse, which also doubled as the church on Sundays. Worse yet, one corner of the roof had developed a small, but steady leak.

"He can't read—not yet, anyway. He's very proud. He's a good friend of ours. And—oh, yes—did I mention that he has four legs and a tail?"

"Prince!" Little Burl screeched, as the other students broke into applause.

"Exactly. I thought we'd write him a letter telling him how much we miss him," Christy said. "Of course, we can't afford to send seventy letters. But you each can write one line. That should only take up a couple of pages. Then we'll send that along with Mr. Pentland to the farm where Prince lives."

Ruby Mae's hand shot up. "I don't rightly see the point, if'n you don't mind my sayin' so. I mean, it's like you said yourself, Miz Christy. Prince can't exactly read." She shrugged. "Who knows? Mr. Collins might even just throw the letter away."

Instantly, Christy thought back to the blanket and bridle she'd rescued from the trash heap the day of the auction. Fortunately, she'd managed to keep Mr. Collins' thoughtless act from Ruby Mae. When they'd arrived home that evening, Christy had hidden the items in the trunk in her bedroom.

"This letter isn't so much for Prince as it is for all of us, Ruby Mae," Christy explained. "I think we've all been feeling sad since Prince's sale. And sometimes it helps to write down your feelings."

"Are you sad, Teacher?" Creed asked.

"Very sad, Creed," Christy answered truthfully.

"Don't know why," Ruby Mae muttered. "You got your money, after all."

"It's true, the mission has been able to buy badly needed medicine and supplies. But that doesn't mean I don't miss Prince."

Christy retrieved two precious pieces of paper from her desk. "I'll start the letter," she said. In her careful penmanship, she wrote at the top of the page:

Dear Prince,

I miss seeing you run in the morning mist. I hope you are happy and eating lots of clover.

Miss Huddleston

She held up the paper. "I want each of you to write down a small note just like this, then sign your name. The older students can help the younger ones if they have trouble."

Christy passed the page to Creed. "While Creed writes his letter to Prince, the rest of you can go on with your lessons."

During the morning, the children worked

on their letter. At first they were very quiet, but soon, as Christy had hoped, they began to exchange happy memories about Prince. The conversation grew more animated, and even though a few tears fell, there was plenty of laughter, too. All in all, Christy decided, her idea was a success. At least she'd given the children an opportunity to express their sadness, and that was a start.

After school let out for the day, Christy sat alone at her desk. After addressing the envelope, she re-read the letter the children had composed. Some of the entries made her laugh out loud. Others made her heart ache:

I miss the way you flik off fliz with yer tal.
Creed Allen

Ridin on yoo, I felt jest lik a hawk in the sky.
Wanda Beck

I miss your wild beauty as you ran through the fields.
Rob Allen

Yer eazee to talk 2.
Mountie O'Teale

I mis the wa yu lovd everbodee. Even me.
Lundy Taylor

Even Ruby Mae had relented and added a note, although hers was very brief:

I love you.
Ruby Mae

Well, Christy thought as she folded up the letter and placed it in the envelope, *their spelling needs plenty of work, but not their hearts.*

"Howdy, Miz Huddleston." Ben Pentland, the mailman, appeared in the doorway, dripping wet.

"Mr. Pentland! Come on in and dry yourself off. You must be freezing."

The tall, weathered man removed his hat and stepped inside the schoolroom. He had a long, slim face, creased by wind and weather, and bushy eyebrows that arched above deep-set eyes. Carefully, he set down his mailbag.

"I've got a letter for you, Miz Huddleston, all the way from Asheville." He fished inside the bag, then handed an ivory envelope to Christy.

"It's from my mother," she said, smiling at the curly handwriting. "And as it happens, I have a letter for you."

Mr. Pentland examined the address. "But . . . I don't mean to pry, Miz Huddleston, but ain't this letter to a . . . well, a *horse?*"

"The children miss Prince so much. I know it seems silly, but I thought perhaps if we

41

wrote him, it would ease their pain a little. Can it be delivered?"

"Sure can. The U-nited States Postal Service aims to please. I'll make sure that letter gets delivered." His eyes twinkled. "'Course, I can't guarantee it'll get *read,* mind you."

"Thank you, Mr. Pentland." Christy hesitated. "Do you know anything about the folks at Great Oak Farm?"

The mailman shrugged. "It's a fancy enough place. 'Course, I don't deliver mail thataways, but I know the fella who does. Hank Drew's his name."

"Maybe you could ask him . . . I mean, if it's no trouble—"

"To check up on ol' Prince? I'd be happy to. Hank's a bit of a busybody, anyway."

"Thank you. It'd be nice, just to know how things are going."

"You frettin' about Prince's new owner?"

"I'm sure Mr. Collins is a fine man," Christy said. "It's just that I want to be sure Prince is adjusting to his new life. That's all. To put the children's minds at ease."

And my own, she added silently.

❧ Seven ❧

❧ Seven ❧

That evening, Christy sat in the mission parlor by a crackling fire and began to write in her diary. She'd filled the pages with her hopes and fears, her embarrassing moments, and her happy ones. Writing down her feelings helped her understand what was happening in her life—the same thing she'd hoped to accomplish today by having the children write a letter to Prince.

Tonight, Prince was very much in her thoughts:

I'm not sure why I can't get that image of Mr. Collins out of my mind—the memory of him tossing aside the blanket and bridle. He's a wealthy man, after all. Perhaps he couldn't see the point in keeping the children's handiwork. To me, those items are worth more than all the riches a man like Mr. Collins possesses, because they're gifts from the heart.

What troubles me most was that he'd promised he would take the items. Was he lying? Or was he just trying to be kind to Ruby Mae? Perhaps, when we were gone, he figured there would be no harm in getting rid of the blanket and bridle. After all, he probably assumed he'd never see us again.

Maybe I'm making too much of this. He was very kind to Prince and Ruby Mae before that. It's just that there was something about his smile . . . something insincere.

Listen to me. I'm letting my imagination get carried away again! Sometimes I think I should be a writer instead of a teacher, the way I'm always making up stories.

Christy paused when she heard someone come into the parlor.

"Am I interruptin'?" Ruby Mae asked. She was dressed in her flannel nightgown and wearing a pair of floppy, hand-me-down socks.

"Not at all. I'd be glad for the company."

"What you writin'?"

"Actually, I was just writing about Prince. I miss him a lot."

Ruby Mae sat next to Christy on the sofa. "Me too. Does the hurtin' ever get any easier, Miz Christy?"

"Time's a great healer. You'll see."

"Maybe." Ruby Mae didn't sound convinced. "It just seems like sometimes I can't get my mind off him. You know?"

"I have an idea." Christy set her diary aside. From her skirt pocket, she retrieved the letter from her mother. She passed the crisp envelope to Ruby Mae. "This is a letter from my mother that Mr. Pentland brought today. I was saving it to read this evening. Why don't you open it, and we'll read it together?"

"Me?" Ruby Mae's eyes glowed. "Open a real, for-true letter?"

"You can read it out loud. It'll be good practice."

Ruby Mae ran her finger over the sealing wax on the back of the letter, embossed with the letter *H*. "Is *H* for Huddleston?"

"That's right. Just slip your fingernail under the seal and the envelope will open."

"Oh, but I just can't, Miz Christy. It's way too purty."

"Go ahead, Ruby Mae. How else will I know what the letter says?"

"When we're done, can I keep the envelope for my own?"

"Sure."

Slowly, carefully, Ruby opened the envelope and withdrew a piece of thick, ivory stationery.

"Look at how purty your ma writes!" Ruby

Mae exclaimed. "All those curlicues like a piglet's tail!"

"I know you're just starting to learn to read cursive writing," Christy said. "Whenever you come to a word you can't figure out, you just tell me."

Ruby Mae cleared her throat and sat up very straight. "'Dearest Christy,'" she began. She grinned. "Guess your ma don't have no cause to call you *Miz.*"

Again she cleared her throat. "'I can't tell you how much your feather and I—'"

"That's probably *father,* Ruby Mae."

"Oops. Yes'm. I do believe it is. Less'n your ma's married to a feather duster." Ruby Mae took a deep breath.

"'—how much your father and I miss you, even after these many months. I find myself talking about you every chance I get. Why, just last Sunday at church, I was telling the editor of the *Asheville C—'*" Ruby Mae frowned. *"C—C—"*

"Sound it out," Christy advised.

"Cou . . . cuckoo?" Ruby asked hopefully.

"*Courier.* It's the Asheville newspaper."

"'I was telling the editor of the *Asheville Courier* all about your adventures, and the interesting people you've met.'"

Ruby Mae glanced at Christy. "Do you ever talk about me, Miz Christy?"

"Of course. You're one of Cutter Gap's most interesting characters."

"How about that! Me, a character!"

"Ruby Mae—the letter."

"Oh. I plumb forgot. Let's see . . . 'He said he'd love to do an article about you, but Cutter Gap is so re . . . remote . . . he just couldn't afford to send a reporter. So I suggested you become a reporter for him and send him articles about your life in Cutter Gap, since you're such a fine writer. And he thought it was a splendid idea.'"

Ruby Mae gasped. "Miz Christy! You could write stories about us for a real newspaper! Wouldn't that just be amazin'? Why, we'd be famous!"

"Oh, I couldn't," Christy protested. "I mean, I'm a teacher, not a writer."

"You write things in your diary most every day."

"But that's different. That's just for me. Besides, who would want to read about my life in Cutter Gap?"

Ruby Mae looked crestfallen. "I s'pose you're right. Those rich people in Asheville don't give a hoot about folks like us."

"Oh, Ruby Mae. That's not what I meant at all!" Christy cried. "It's just that I'm no reporter. I wouldn't know how to describe my life here. I wouldn't be able to do it justice."

"I know what you mean," Ruby Mae said quietly. "It's like today, when you asked us to write Prince how we was feelin'. I thought and thought, but I just couldn't find the right words."

"But you did. You wrote exactly the right words. Three of them, to be exact."

"So how come you couldn't do it, too?"

"This is different. The paper's going to want more than three words."

"So fancy 'em up a bit."

Christy shook her head. "I don't think so, Ruby Mae."

"Fine. Guess I won't get to be famous, after all."

"Oh, I have no doubt you'll be famous someday, Ruby Mae," Christy smiled, "but there's plenty of time for that."

❧ Eight ❧

Three weeks after Prince's sale, Mr. Pentland came to the door of the mission house. "Special delivery from the U-nited States Postal Service!"

"Mr. Pentland," Christy cried, "look at all these boxes! What have you brought us?"

He pointed to the load of crates on his small wagon. "Looks like supplies, unless I miss my guess. All I can tell you is some of them is right heavy."

Miss Alice, David, and Miss Ida came to the door. "My, you *are* a welcome sight, Ben Pentland!" Miss Ida exclaimed.

Mr. Pentland blushed. "Just doin' my job, ma'am."

"We have Prince to thank for this bounty," Miss Alice said.

"Without that money, we wouldn't have been able to buy these supplies."

"That reminds me, Mr. Pentland," Christy said. "Do you know if the children's letter to Prince was safely delivered? It's only been about two weeks since we sent it, but still, I was hoping for a reply of some kind."

David winked at Christy. "He's a fine horse," he said, "but as far as I know, his penmanship is lousy."

"I *meant* from Mr. Collins," Christy said, grinning. "Of course, he's probably too busy . . ."

"There's somethin' I need to be tellin' you folks, much as it pains me," Mr. Pentland said. He hefted a crate off the cart and set it on the ground, then paused.

"What is it, Mr. Pentland?" Christy asked.

The mailman stroked his chin. "Guess there ain't any good way to say this. I ran into Hank Drew yesterday mornin' over at the general store in El Pano. He's the one I told you about, Miz Huddleston, the mailman over to those parts."

"The one who delivers mail to Great Oak Farm?" Christy asked.

"Yep. I asked Hank about the letter to Prince, seein' as how it was a mighty unusual piece o' deliverin'. I've delivered plenty of mail in my time, but I can tell you for sure and certain I ain't never delivered mail to no horse! To any critter, come to think of it."

Christy nodded patiently. Mr. Pentland didn't talk much, but when he did, he had a slow, deliberate way of getting to the point.

"Anyways, Hank and me got to talkin', and he said he gave one of the stable hands—Uriah was his name, I think—the letter." Mr. Pentland offered Christy an apologetic look. "This Uriah fella just up and laughed and crumpled the letter up in a ball. Said maybe Prince'd want to eat it."

"Well, I suppose I should have expected that," Christy said sadly. "After all, the point of the letter was to make the children feel better."

Mr. Pentland cleared his throat. "Thing is, that ain't the whole of it, Miz Huddleston. Seems Uriah told Hank that Prince has been nothin' but trouble since the day they bought him. Ran away twice, he said."

"I'm not really surprised," David said grimly. "Prince always has had a mind of his own."

"It'd be bad enough, the runnin' away," Mr. Pentland said. "But Hank told me as he was leavin', he heard the sound of a whip, crackin' away like thunder. A man was screamin' and carryin' on. And a frightened horse was stomping and whinnying something fierce." He shook his head. "It was Prince. One of the stable hands was beatin' him like there was no tomorrow."

"Oh, no!" Christy cried.

David clenched his fists in fury. "I'll . . . I'll go straight to that Collins, and I'll give him a piece of my mind. Why, I ought to—"

"David," Miss Alice interrupted, "calm down. We're all upset to hear that Prince is being treated badly. But uttering idle threats isn't going to help."

"They *aren't* idle!" David shouted. "I've got half a mind to give that man a taste of his own medicine."

"The sad truth is, Jared Collins is Prince's owner," Miss Alice said. "There's not a whole lot we can do about this. Except, perhaps, to appeal to Mr. Collins' better nature."

"You're going to try to reason with him?" David demanded. "A lot of good that will do. You can't reason with a man like that."

"Perhaps Mr. Collins doesn't know about the way the stable hands are treating Prince," Miss Alice suggested. "Right now, we're leaping to conclusions."

"I'm not so sure, Miss Alice," Christy said. "Maybe I should have seen this coming."

"You?" she asked. "Why?"

"Right after we sold Prince, I saw Mr. Collins throw away Lundy's bridle and the blanket the children made for Prince. I went back and saved them." Christy shook her head. "I know Mr. Collins is a wealthy man and those things must have seemed very crude to him, but there was something so . . . cruel and callous about the way he tossed them aside. It made me worry at the time. Now I see that I should have worried more."

"All the more reason for me to confront him, man to man," David said, his jaw clenched.

Miss Alice put a calming hand on David's shoulder. "David, you know that I, as a Quaker, believe in non-violence. You also know that one of the first things I did when I came to Cutter Gap was buy a gun and learn to shoot it." She chuckled. "No doubt I've had my dear ancestors spinning in their graves ever since."

"Well, I've never seen a better time to use a gun than now," David snapped.

"I'm a better shot than a lot of men in this Cove. And because they know it and respect it, it's given me a base for talking straight to them," Miss Alice said. "But now that I've lived here a while and seen violence close up, I believe in non-violence more than ever."

"Miss Alice is right, David," Christy said. "Threatening Mr. Collins won't help. According to the law, Prince belongs to him."

"So that gives him the right to harm a beautiful, living creature? What about God's law?"

His question hung in the air. "I don't have an easy answer, David," Miss Alice finally said. "But I'll be heading over toward El Pano at the end of the week to check on Kettie Weller's new twins. Why don't I pay Mr. Collins a visit and see what can be done for Prince?"

David frowned. "If it's all the same to you, Miss Alice, I'd rather go myself."

"I don't think that's a good idea," she replied. "You're too upset about this right now. Besides, you've got your work cut out for you here, fixing that leak in the schoolhouse roof."

"I'd like to go along," Christy volunteered. "That is, if David doesn't mind watching the children that day."

"Go ahead," David said resignedly. "Miss Alice is right. The way I feel right now, I'd probably do more harm than good." He gave a self-conscious smile. "Look at me! Some minister, huh? I get angry about something, and my first reaction is to lash out."

"You're only human, David," Christy said.

"Then it's settled," Miss Alice said. "We'll talk to Mr. Collins and see what happens. All we can do is take this one step at a time."

"And in the meantime," David said darkly, "Prince is the one who suffers."

❧ Nine ❧

What are you going to say to Mr. Collins when we get there?" Christy asked Miss Alice later that week.

They were almost to Great Oak Farm. The day was overcast and damp, and Christy's legs ached from the long walk to El Pano. They'd taken turns riding Goldie, Miss Alice's horse, and last night they'd rested at Kettie Weller's cabin, but it was still an exhausting trip. Nonetheless, Christy was glad she'd come. Somehow, she felt she owed this much to Prince.

"I'm not sure what I'll say to Mr. Collins," Miss Alice said, bending down to pat Goldie's glistening mane. "But I'm sure the Lord will help me find the words."

"You always do seem to know just the right thing to say. I'll bet you would have made a fine writer, Miss Alice," Christy smiled, ". . . or a preacher."

"I wouldn't have the patience to put words on paper," Miss Alice replied. "And as for preaching, I'm ministering the way I love best—doing a little bit of everything. Teaching, doctoring, you name it. I suppose you could say I'm a jack-of-all-trades."

Christy lifted her long skirt to step over a fallen log. "You know, I got a letter from my mother not long ago. She said the editor of the newspaper back home in Asheville had suggested I write about my experiences here in Cutter Gap."

"And what was your response?"

"I told her to tell him I was flattered, but that I didn't think I'd be very good at it."

Miss Alice shook a finger at Christy. "You'd be good at anything you set your mind to, Christy Huddleston. I truly believe that." She paused. "Although in this case, you probably made the right decision. The people of Cutter Gap are a proud lot—proud and terribly private. I'm not sure how they'd take to the notion of your writing about them."

"I tried to start an article," Christy admitted. "You know—just to see if I could do it." She shrugged. "Actually, I was just writing in my diary, and it sort of turned into a piece about Prince, and all he'd meant to the children. But after everything that happened with him, I couldn't find the heart to finish it."

They came to a fork in the path. On the right, the path broadened into a wide, dirt road. "Another half-mile or so up that road, and we'll be to Great Oak Farm," Christy said.

"You know, I'd like to read that story about Prince sometime, if you feel like sharing it," Miss Alice said.

"I'll think about it. But first, let's see if it's going to have a happy ending."

———

"Well, it's a beautiful farm," Miss Alice said. "I'll give it that much."

Christy surveyed the manicured lawn and immaculate stables. The imposing white house was a few hundred yards from the stables. A broad path lined in stately oaks led to the front porch. "Should we go knock on the front door?"

Miss Alice dismounted and tied Goldie to a nearby tree. "We're here to visit Prince," she said firmly. "Better to arrive unexpected and see how he's doing first. Then we'll say hello to Mr. Collins."

They started for the largest barn. In the fenced-off field in the distance, several beautiful horses grazed contentedly. "They look happy enough," Christy whispered to Miss Alice. "Maybe Mr. Pentland's friend was wrong. Maybe this is all some terrible mistake." But even to her own ears, her words sounded hollow.

The barn was cool and quiet, filled with the sweet scent of hay. Most of the stalls were empty, and there were no stable hands in sight. Christy and Miss Alice walked slowly down the aisle, taking in the brass name plates on the door. *Rebel. Jericho. Long Shot.*

And then, there it was: *Prince.*

Christy ran her fingers over the engraved name. Suddenly, a terrible noise met her ears—the heart-breaking sound of an animal in pain.

"Prince!" Christy cried. "That's him, I know it is!"

She ran down the aisle to the end of the barn, with Miss Alice close on her heels. At the open door, they stopped short.

In a nearby paddock stood four men. Prince was in the middle of the paddock. His mouth was foaming. His coat was slick with sweat.

"Told you he can't be ridden." One of the men spat in disgust. "If I didn't know better, I'd swear he ain't saddle-broke."

"I'll show him who's boss," another man said.

Christy grabbed Miss Alice's arm. "That's

Uriah Wynne," she said, "the stable hand at the auction."

Uriah grabbed a whip and coiled it in his right hand. Slowly he approached Prince, talking to him under his breath. "You better mind me, boy, or you'll be worm food before I'm through with you," he muttered.

With each step closer, Prince grew more agitated. His ears flickered wildly, and his eyes were wide with fear. Suddenly, he reared up, his great hooves flailing in the air, towering over Uriah.

Crack! In a flash, Uriah let loose the whip. It caught Prince on his right shoulder, and the stallion leapt back in shock.

Again Uriah let the leather whip fly. The whip cracked, and the stallion reared up in pain.

"I don't care what it takes," Christy cried in horror. "I've got to find a way to get Prince away from here!"

❧ Ten ❧

Stop it!" Christy screamed, dashing to the fence. "Stop it, now! You're hurting him!"

"Well, looky here," one of the men said. "We got ourselves some lady visitors."

Miss Alice strode up calmly. "Prince," she said in a soothing voice. "Calm down, boy."

Prince lowered his front hooves. He jerked his head in confusion.

Miss Alice clucked her tongue, and in an instant, Prince seemed to recognize her. Slowly, nervously, he approached them. Christy leaned over the fence and embraced his neck while Miss Alice stroked his ears.

"This is a fine horse, gentlemen," Miss Alice said in a stern voice. "But like all animals, he responds better to kindness than to threats."

"Is that so?" Uriah swaggered over, tapping

the whip handle in his palm. "And just who are you to be tellin' us our business, lady?"

"Uriah!" came a sharp voice. "That will be enough."

Striding toward the paddock came Jared Collins. He was wearing a starched white shirt, riding breeches, and tall, black leather riding boots.

With a gracious smile, he bowed low to Christy. "This young lady is Miss Christy Huddleston from the Cutter Gap mission," he said to Uriah, "and to my great delight, our most welcome guest." He turned to Miss Alice. "Jared Collins, at your service. And you might be?"

"Alice Henderson," Miss Alice said coolly.

"How can you sit there introducing yourself like nothing's wrong?" Christy demanded, rounding on Mr. Collins. "Didn't you see? He—he was beating Prince! How can you let someone like this work for you?"

"Uriah is one of my most trusted hands. He's worked with horses since he was just a boy. I'm sure you're misinterpreting events, Miss Huddleston."

"Misinterpreting?" Christy cried in fury. "He beat him with a whip! You could have heard Prince in the next county, he was in so much pain!"

"The use of a whip when training horses is not at all uncommon," Mr. Collins said, favoring Christy with a tolerant smile. "In fact, it's often recommended for a horse with Prince's—shall we say—difficult temperament."

Miss Alice cleared her throat. "Mr. Collins, I can tell you with some authority that Prince does not have a difficult temperament. Quite the contrary. When treated with respect and love, he responds beautifully to commands. Certainly he's strong-willed, but with a knowledgeable rider—"

"I assure you, Madam, I am an accomplished equestrian."

"Then you know," Miss Alice continued in her calm, deliberate way, "that a horse who has learned to fear is a horse who cannot be managed."

"In my experience, fear leads to respect."

"I know ten-year-old girls who can handle that horse better than your men," Miss Alice said, "and they do it with love."

"I own dozens of horses, Madam," Mr. Collins said dismissively. "I don't have time for—" he sneered, "love. Besides, look around you. This is the finest horse farm in seven counties. Prince has everything a stallion could ask for. The finest care, the finest food, the finest pasture."

Christy rubbed her cheek against Prince's hot, damp neck. "All I know is, I've never seen him like this. He's afraid. He's unhappy."

"He's merely untrained and ill-mannered,"

Mr. Collins said. "When a horse won't respond to a rider of my impeccable training, the problem, dear lady, lies with the horse."

For a moment, no one spoke. Uriah spat on the ground. Far off in the distance, a horse whinnied softly.

"Mr. Collins," Miss Alice said at last, "we may differ on how to care for a horse like Prince. But there's one thing I think we can agree on—he's a fine animal."

"Indeed. On that we do agree."

"Perhaps you're right, and the problem lies in the way Prince has been trained. If that's the case, we both know it's probably too late to change him. Suppose we agree that things haven't worked out? The mission will take him off your hands, and return your money in full as soon as we can manage it."

Christy nearly gasped. How could Miss Alice make such an offer? Where would the mission ever get the money to repay Mr. Collins?

Mr. Collins tried to pat Prince on the shoulder, but the horse moved out of his reach. "Thank you for your offer, Miss Henderson. It's very generous of you. But this horse belongs to me, and I intend to keep him. As a matter of fact, I intend to be riding him before the month is out." He gave an icy smile. "Perhaps I'll ride by your dark little corner of the world and show you how it's done. It's really very simple. With a dumb animal like this, you just have to show him who's boss." He bowed. "Now, if you'll excuse me, I have other matters to attend to. I'm sure you can find your way out."

———

"I still can't believe you offered to buy Prince back," Christy said that afternoon as she and Miss Alice headed back to Cutter Gap.

Miss Alice sighed. "It was worth a try."

"But where would we have found the money?"

"The Lord has a way of providing."

"Did you—" Christy glanced over her shoulder. "Did you hear something just now? Behind us, I mean?"

"You're just tired. Why don't you ride Goldie for a while? It's your turn."

"I'm fine. I just thought I heard someone following us." Christy shook her head. "Every time I close my eyes, I hear Prince crying out in pain. Miss Alice, isn't there something else we can do?"

"I gave Mr. Collins our address," Miss Alice reminded her, "and I told him to contact us immediately if he decides Prince is too much trouble. I don't know what we can do beyond that."

"It's so unfair," Christy groaned. "Owning an animal doesn't give you a license to mistreat it. I just feel so . . . so hopeless."

"Whatever you do, Christy, you must never give up hope." Miss Alice looked down at her with her warm, tender gaze, and somehow Christy felt better. "For now, we'll pray for Prince's well-being, and that God will provide a way for us to solve this problem. In the meantime, promise me you won't stop hoping. Who knows what tomorrow may bring?"

◈ Eleven ◈

That night, Christy lay in her bed, exhausted, sore, and dejected.

She had blisters on both her feet. Her leg muscles had turned to hard knots. Her face was chapped from the cold, wet air. But it was her heart that was truly hurting.

She opened her diary and stared at the single sentence she'd written after coming home:

How could we have abandoned Prince?

But of course, they'd had no choice. Prince belonged to Mr. Collins, and that was that.

Perhaps they could have gone to the local sheriff and complained about Prince's mistreatment. But Christy knew that would have been pointless. These mountains were ruled by guns. This was a place where women and children could be horribly mistreated, and no one—not even the law—would lift a finger to help them. Nobody in these parts had the time to worry about a mistreated horse. Especially when the horse was living at Great Oak Farm, the finest farm for miles around.

Christy turned to the story about Prince that she'd mentioned to Miss Alice. It began:

> *He's just a horse, some would say. Four sturdy legs. A shiny mane. An insatiable taste for sugar.*
>
> *But I know better. I've seen the little miracles.*
>
> *Around Prince, the little girl who stutters somehow speaks with ease.*
>
> *Around Prince, the vicious bully turns gentle and protective.*
>
> *Around Prince, the child set apart by the color of her skin becomes a friend at last.*
>
> *He may be just a horse, but try telling that to my seventy Cutter Gap students.*

With a heavy sigh, Christy closed her diary. There was no point in reading on. Prince's story did not have a happy ending, after all.

Christy put out the light and closed her

eyes. But every time she started to drift off, she imagined she could hear Prince. Sometimes it was just his familiar, soft nicker. Other times it was the horrifying whinny of terror and pain she'd heard today at the farm.

Soon another noise drifted into her awareness. *Tap, tap, tap.*

"Miz Christy?"

The muffled voice had to belong to Ruby Mae. Christy climbed out of bed, threw on her robe to ward off the chill, and opened the door.

Ruby Mae was standing in the dark hallway. Her face was in shadow, but there was just enough moonlight spilling from Christy's window to illuminate Ruby Mae's huge grin.

"I got a surprise for you," Ruby Mae said. She was wearing her worn, wool coat over her nightgown. Her feet were bare.

"It had better be a good surprise, at this time of night," Christy replied.

"I'll give you some hints," Ruby Mae whispered loudly. "He can't read—not yet, anyway. He's very proud. He's a good friend of ours. Let's see what else. Oops. Almost forgot. He's got four legs and a mighty fine tail."

Christy grabbed Ruby Mae by the shoulders and pulled her into the room. "Ruby Mae, I want you to wake up," she commanded. "I think you're sleepwalking."

Ruby Mae leapt onto Christy's bed, laughing gaily. "Not hardly." She pinched her arm. "See? I'm as awake as can be, Miz Christy."

"All right. Start over. Tell me exactly what you're talking about," Christy said as she lit her lamp.

"You won't believe me even if I tell you. How about I *show* you what I'm talkin' about? Then you'll know I ain't a-dreamin'."

Christy put on her slippers. "Fine, then. You can show me. But after that, you're going straight to bed so you can finish this nice dream—or whatever it is."

Ruby Mae grabbed Christy's hand and led her down the staircase. The mission house was still, except for the soft sound of snoring drifting down from Miss Ida's room.

Outside, the wind was brisk and the sky was crowded with dazzling stars. "Shouldn't you go put on some shoes?" Christy asked, hesitating on the porch.

"I'm so excited I can't feel a thing!" Ruby Mae exclaimed. "Come on, Miz Christy! Hurry!"

Ruby Mae dashed across the dark lawn toward the little stable that housed the mission's animals. It was just an overgrown shed that David had built with bits and pieces of leftover lumber, but at least it provided shelter from the weather.

Shivering, Christy hurried toward the stable.

When she was closer, she could hear Ruby Mae chattering away inside.

"Ruby Mae, I really wish you'd tell me what this is about," Christy said as she reached the doorway. But even before she'd spoken the words, she had her answer.

"Prince!" Christy gasped.

"Told you! Ain't it a plumb fine miracle, Miz Christy?" Ruby Mae said, beaming. She planted a kiss on Prince's nose. He responded with a polite attempt to eat her hair.

"But . . . but how . . ."

"All I know is, I was havin' a wonderful dream that Prince had come back. All of a sudden I clean woke up, and sure as shootin', I coulda swore I heard him nickerin' below my window. So I went and looked, and who do you think I saw?"

Christy scratched the great stallion's ear. "He must have found his way home. You know, I *thought* I heard someone following us on our way back from Mr. Collins'. You don't think he escaped from Great Oak Farm and followed us, do you?"

"Prince is smarter than a whole passel o' humans. I wouldn't be surprised if you told me he could recite the alphabet backwards."

Christy laughed, but Ruby Mae's expression grew grave. "Miz Christy, you ain't a-goin' to make him go back, are you? He come all this way 'cause it's us he wants to be with."

"He belongs to Mr. Collins, Ruby Mae. I don't see how we can keep him."

But I don't see how we can send him back, either, she added silently. *Not after what Miss Alice and I saw today.*

Ruby Mae thought for a while. "I'm stayin' with him tonight. Could be it's the last night Prince'll be here."

"Ruby Mae, you can't. You'll catch cold out here. It's freezing."

"I'm stayin', and that's all there is to it."

Christy knew all too well the determined look on Ruby Mae's face. She also knew it was pointless to argue with her.

"I'll go get some blankets and some warm clothes for both of us," Christy said at last.

"Both of us?"

"I'm not letting you stay out here by yourself, Ruby Mae." Christy smiled at Prince. "After all, he's my friend, too."

❧ Twelve ❧

"Have you ever seen them so happy?"
Christy asked the next day.

Christy, David, and Miss Alice were standing
in the yard outside the schoolhouse during the
noon break. Nearby, Ruby Mae and Hannah
were leading Prince in slow circles, giving rides
to the younger children.

"It's like a party," David agreed, "and look
at Prince. You can tell he loves being the
center of attention again."

Miss Alice shook her head. "I still can't
believe he found his way home. It's quite
amazing."

They watched as Prince came to a halt.
Carefully, Ruby Mae helped Little Burl down
off the stallion. Mountie, who was next in
line for a ride, smiled gleefully as Hannah
helped her aboard Prince's broad back.

"I missed you, Prince," Mountie said in a clear, joyful voice. "I sure am glad you decided to come visit for a spell."

Christy glanced at David, then looked away. That, of course, was the question—how long would Prince be a part of their lives this time?

"I don't see how we can take him back to Great Oak," David said, "knowing what we know. It just wouldn't be fair."

"He doesn't belong to us, David," Miss Alice reminded him. "He's still the property of Jared Collins."

"Maybe if we just stall for a while," Christy suggested. "We might come up with a solution, if we just give it some time. At least—" she lowered her voice as some of the children ran past, "at least we'll know Prince is safe, for the time being."

Miss Alice leaned against an oak tree, watching Hannah lead Prince around the yard. "Stalling is hardly a solution," she said.

"I know," Christy sighed. "But what else *can* we do?"

"I'll tell you one thing," David said firmly. "I am not going to be part of any decision to send Prince back to Great Oak Farm. When I think of him being whipped and abused, it just makes my blood boil—"

"David. Shh." Christy grabbed his arm. "Ruby Mae is coming—"

"Hello, Ruby Mae," David said cheerfully, spinning around to greet her, "and what can we do for you?"

Ruby Mae cocked her head to one side, eyeing him doubtfully. "Who got whopped?"

"Ruby Mae, that conversation was between David and Miss Alice and me," Christy interjected. "You have no right to be eavesdropping."

But Ruby Mae was determined. "This is about Prince, ain't it?" she demanded, her expression hardening. "He done got hisself whopped over at Great Oak, didn't he?"

"This doesn't concern you, Ruby Mae," David said wearily.

Ruby Mae planted her hands on her hips. "Was they treatin' him bad over at that fancy farm?" she cried. "I'll bet that's how come he run away!" She frowned at Christy. "We stayed with him all last night, and you didn't even tell me! And you call yourself his friend?"

Christy rubbed her eyes. "There wasn't any point in worrying you, Ruby Mae. And it doesn't seem like there's anything we can do. Prince belongs to Mr. Collins—"

"So that makes it all right to hurt him?"

"No, of course not. But—"

"So what are you plannin' now? You goin' to give him back, like a cup o' sugar you borrowed? Send him back to those bad people like nothin's wrong?"

Ruby Mae didn't wait for an answer. She stomped off across the lawn, her red hair flying.

"So what *are* we planning?" David asked softly.

Christy shrugged. "Let's just say we're hoping for divine guidance. The sooner, the better."

— — —

That night, Christy awoke to the sound of the downstairs door closing. She sat up in bed, alert and listening. Were those footsteps she'd heard, or was it just the wind?

Cautiously, she tiptoed down the stairway. Her lamp spread a golden glow over the dark house.

"Miss Ida?" she asked, but the only answer was the sound of a branch creaking outside.

Christy checked the door and scanned the parlor. Nothing. With a sigh, she headed back upstairs. She was probably just imagining things. Of course, last night Ruby Mae had imagined that she'd heard a horse outside her window—and she'd been right!

When she passed Ruby Mae's door, Christy peeked inside. Ruby Mae was sound asleep, snoring softly and looking angelic. Christy smiled. Children always looked so peaceful and innocent when they were asleep.

Quietly, Christy closed Ruby Mae's door.

It was a shame Ruby Mae had overheard David's comment today. There was no point whatsoever in worrying the children about Prince. They had enough pain to deal with every day.

It wasn't until she was climbing into bed that Christy realized something hadn't quite been right with the angelic impression she'd had of Ruby Mae. Was she imagining things, or had one of Ruby Mae's feet been sticking out from the covers—and wearing a *shoe?*

Curious, Christy returned to Ruby Mae's room and cracked open the door.

Ruby Mae's shoes were on the floor. Both of them.

Christy yawned. Once again, her imagination was getting the better of her.

❧ Thirteen ❧

He's gone," David said the next morning when Christy came downstairs.

Christy blinked, taking in the scene in the dining room. David was sitting at the table with Miss Ida and Miss Alice. All of them looked grim. Apparently, Ruby Mae wasn't awake yet.

"Who's gone?" Christy asked, but the look on David's face told her all she needed to know.

"Prince." David combed fingers through his tousled hair. "Vanished, without a trace. I followed some tracks, but I lost them in the woods after about a quarter-mile."

Christy took a seat at the table. "What do you think happened?"

"Could be he ran away, but I doubt it. The latch on his stall was secure last night. I checked it before I went to bed."

Miss Ida poured Christy a cup of tea. "Maybe that awful Mr. Collins tracked him down and took Prince back."

"It's possible," Miss Alice said, "but in the middle of the night?"

"Besides, if Collins had found Prince here, he would have confronted us about it, I'd think." David leaned back in his chair, arms crossed over his chest. "Of course, there are other possibilities."

"Do you mean that terrible Lyle Duster and his brother Ed might have stolen Prince?"

David looked surprised, then thoughtful. "That's always a possibility," he admitted. "Actually, I was thinking that our problem may lie closer to home. Somebody who loves Prince may have hidden him to protect him," David replied.

Just then, Ruby Mae sauntered down the stairs. She yawned, stretched her arms out over her head, and grinned. "Mornin'. Everybody sleep all right?"

"Actually," Christy said, "I had some trouble sleeping. I thought I heard someone come into the house late last night, so I came downstairs to check."

"Probably just the wind," Ruby Mae said, looking away. She reached for a piece of toast and took her seat next to Christy. "It was mighty windy last night."

"Oh?" Christy asked. "Were you up, too?"

"Me? I just got woke up by the wind noise, same as you. Only for a minute. The rest o' the night, I slept just like a babe."

Everyone watched in silence as Ruby Mae gobbled down her toast and reached for another piece.

"What?" she demanded. "Why in tarnation is everybody starin' at me? Was I talkin' with my mouth full again?"

"Ruby Mae," Miss Alice said, "Prince is missing."

Ruby Mae's jaw went slack. She dropped her toast into her lap. "You mean—you mean they done took him back?"

"We're not sure *what* to think," Christy said. "Do you have any idea what might have happened to him?"

"Well . . ." Ruby Mae retrieved her toast and took a bite while she considered the question. "I s'pose he coulda run back to Great Oak all on his own, but that don't seem likely."

"No," David agreed, "it doesn't."

"Or them awful, sneaky men at the auction could o' made off with him." David and Christy exchanged glances.

"Or," Ruby Mae continued, "he could be hidin' somewheres on account o' he's afraid o' goin' back."

"All on his own?" Christy asked.

"You know, Miz Christy, he's a right smart horse."

"Not that smart."

Ruby Mae gulped down the rest of her toast and leapt out of her seat. "Well, I s'pose I ought to be gettin' ready for school. I plumb overslept."

"You know, you don't seem all that upset about Prince's disappearance," David noted.

"Oh, I'm worried, Preacher. But it's like I said—Prince is a right smart horse."

With that, Ruby Mae rushed back up the stairs, taking two steps at a time.

Christy looked at the others. "What do you think?"

"I think," Miss Alice said, "that this problem just keeps getting more and more complicated."

"I think," David added, "that Ruby Mae has great potential as a dramatic actress."

～ ～ ～

"What are you working on, Christy?" Miss Alice asked early that evening.

They were sitting in the parlor by a crackling fire. Christy was curled up on the worn, old sofa, and Miss Alice was seated across from her, sipping on a cup of tea while she stared out the window at the darkening sky.

Christy held up her diary. "I should be working on my lesson plans. But to tell you the truth, I was writing about Prince in my diary. Sometimes, when I write things down, it helps me clarify my thoughts."

"And this time?"

"This time, I'm afraid it's not helping. Miss Alice, the way the children acted today at school, I'm sure they know what happened to Prince. For one thing, there was far too much whispering and note-passing. For another, they hardly mentioned his disappearance. And as if that weren't enough, they were unusually well-behaved."

"So you think after Ruby Mae overheard David, she decided to kidnap Prince?"

"Horse-nap, is more like it. But I'll bet it wasn't just Ruby Mae. I wouldn't be surprised if several of the children were involved."

"A conspiracy, in our very midst. If you're right, they could have hidden him anywhere. In these mountains, it could take months to find him. Years, even."

"If the children took Prince, I'm sure that's what they're hoping." Christy sighed. "The truth is, I wish I knew for sure they took him. It would certainly be a relief to know that Prince is safe. Of course, it also presents another problem: The children need to learn that they can't go around taking other people's property."

"Christy, you're limited in what you can do until you're sure what's really happened. This is turning into quite a messy story." Miss

Alice pointed to Christy's diary. "You know, speaking of stories, you told me a while ago that you might let me read that article about Prince."

"It still doesn't have an ending. And besides, it's really not very good, Miss Alice."

"Why don't you let me be the judge of that?"

Reluctantly, Christy opened her worn diary to the page where her story about Prince began. She passed the book to Miss Alice.

While the fire crackled away, Miss Alice read, smiling occasionally. When she was done, she closed the diary and wiped away a tear.

"That was lovely, Christy. You truly captured the way Prince changed the children's lives." She paused. "I think I was wrong when I said the folks in Cutter Gap might be offended by an article. Why don't you send this to the editor in Asheville? I'll bet he'd be proud to publish it. And I think the children would be honored to see it in print."

"Oh, Miss Alice, I'm not sure I'd have the nerve. Besides, it doesn't have an ending. We don't even know what's happened to Prince."

"I'm not sure it needs an ending. It's beautiful, just the way it is. This is a story about a group of loving children, and the way their love for an animal helped them through some hard times. Whatever happens with Prince, that won't change."

Christy thumbed through the pages of her diary. "I suppose I could send it in. Who knows—the editor might even pay me something for it. And the Lord knows we could use the money."

"Well, that's one thing settled," Miss Alice said. "Now, if we could just decide what to do about our missing horse."

"Let's give the children some time. I have a feeling they'll tell us the truth eventually."

"Let's hope so."

Christy grinned. "A wise woman once told me never to give up hope."

Miss Alice smiled back. "She was right."

❧ Fourteen ❧

"**R**eady or not, it's time for your spelling test," Christy announced one afternoon.

A week and a half had passed since Prince's disappearance. So far, no one had stepped forward to admit any involvement. In fact, the children hardly mentioned Prince at all—a sure sign, in Christy's mind, that they were keeping a very big secret.

"While the test is going on, I want the younger students to practice writing the alphabet on their chalkboards," Christy instructed. "Are the rest of you ready?"

"Ain't never ready for spellin' tests," Creed muttered.

"Actually, spelling is very important, Creed," Christy said as she erased the chalkboard at the front of the room. "If we can't spell correctly, we can't communicate with each other as efficiently. And communicating with each other is very important." She gave the class a meaningful look. "Even when it's very difficult to do."

She perched on the edge of her battered, wooden desk. "All right, then. Your first word is *prince.*"

A low murmur went through the room, but soon the children were concentrating on their small chalkboards. The only sound was the soft *tap-tap-tap* of the chalk as they wrote.

"The next word is," Christy continued, *"honesty."*

She noticed Ruby Mae and Lundy exchanging a glance before they began writing. A few other students looked a little uncomfortable.

"And your next word is *hiding.*"

Ruby Mae grimaced and raised her hand. "Miz Christy? I got a spellin' question for you," she said in an accusing voice. "How do you spell *whoppin'?*"

The other students nodded in agreement. It was clear everyone understood what Ruby Mae really meant.

"Well, that's a good question, Ruby Mae," Christy said guardedly. "And I—"

"Excuse me for interruptin'," came a gruff voice at the doorway.

It was Uriah Wynne, along with two other

stable hands Christy recognized from Great Oak Farm.

"Mr. Wynne!" Christy cried, her heart leaping into her throat. "This really isn't a good time. As you can see, I'm in the middle of teaching a class."

"This won't take but a minute." Uriah stepped into the classroom, leaving his two friends by the door. "I think you know why we're here. We come for Prince."

"Prince," Christy repeated. She cast a glance at the children. They were sitting erect in their seats, silent as stones.

"We know he come here. Word got back to El Pano. Somebody out thisaways said he come runnin' here."

Christy cleared her throat. "Well, you're right, actually. He did come here. He must have followed Miss Alice and me home."

"Broke outa his pen." Uriah started to spit, then thought better of it. "Confounded horse is more trouble than he's worth, if you ask me. But Mr. C won't give up on him. Don't ask me why. He can't ride him, that's for sure." He rubbed his hands together. "So where is he?"

Christy looked at her students. Their faces were grave. No one said a word. No one moved a muscle.

"I wish I could tell you, Mr. Wynne," Christy said, "but the truth is, Prince disappeared not long after he got here. The Reverend Grantland was able to follow his tracks for about a quarter of a mile, but then he lost them in the woods. We haven't seen him since."

Uriah strode toward Christy, his eyes blazing. "Looky here, little lady. I ain't got time for no games. We been lookin' for this horse for way too long, and Mr. C's like to fire us or worse if'n we don't bring him back."

"I'm telling you the truth, Mr. Wynne," Christy said, "and now, if you please, I'd appreciate it if you'd leave my classroom. We have a spelling test to complete."

"Why, I oughta—" Uriah lifted his arm as if he were going to strike Christy.

Instantly, Lundy leapt from his desk. He grabbed Uriah's arm and easily pinned it behind the man's back. "Don't you be threatenin' Teacher, hear?" he growled.

"Git him offa me!" Uriah groaned.

"Lundy, that's enough," Christy instructed. "You may let Mr. Wynne go now."

Reluctantly, Lundy released the man. "Ain't polite to threaten a lady," he muttered.

Christy almost smiled. It wasn't so long ago that Lundy himself had threatened Christy. She supposed this was progress—of a sort.

"I will pass your concerns along, Mr. Wynne," Christy said. "I'm confident that if anyone in Cutter Gap knows of Prince's whereabouts, they'll inform Mr. Collins."

Uriah narrowed his eyes. "We'll be back," he said, shaking a finger at her. "Mr. C ain't the kind to let somethin' like this go. And believe you me, lady, you don't want to go troublin' Mr. C."

When the men had left, Christy straightened her skirt and forced a smile. "I'm sure you were all hoping I'd forget about the spelling test after that little interruption. I'm afraid you're not going to be that fortunate."

The children didn't respond. They were staring at the doorway where Uriah and his friends had just departed.

"Your next word," Christy said forcefully, "is *secret.*"

"I'm thinkin' on another word—" Ruby Mae muttered softly, *"afeared."*

✤ Fifteen ✤

Howdy, Miz Huddleston!"

Christy peeked past the wet bed sheet she was hanging on the clothesline to dry. "Mr. Pentland! How are you this afternoon? It's nice to see some sun for a change."

"Yes'm. Reckon you're right about that." The mailman reached into his bag. "Got a letter for ya. Don't look like it's from your ma, though. Not, of course, that employees of the U-nited States Postal Service would ever snoop into a person's mail, mind you."

"Of course not." Christy accepted the long, white envelope. It wasn't her mother's stationery, and the ink on the return address was blurred.

She started to open it, then hesitated. Could this be from Mr. Collins? More than a week had passed since Uriah had come to

Cutter Gap. But Christy felt certain that the threatening visit hadn't been the end of things.

"Any sign o' Prince?" Mr. Pentland inquired.

"No. Nothing. Have you heard anything?"

Mr. Pentland shook his head. "Heard some talk about Jared Collins sendin' his men over to these parts."

"Yes. They did pay us a visit."

"I reckon they weren't too friendly, neither."

"That would be a fair statement," Christy said as she removed the letter from its envelope.

"Good news, I hope?" Mr. Pentland asked.

"Oh, my!" Christy scanned the address at the top of the letter. "It's from the *Asheville Courier!* This *is* good news! They want to buy an article I wrote!"

"Well, I'll be. Ain't that somethin'? A real live writer, right here in Cutter Gap."

Christy kissed Mr. Pentland on the cheek. "Thank you, Mr. Pentland. This is wonderful news!"

She left the blushing mailman and ran into the mission house. "Miss Ida! Miss Alice! Ruby Mae! David! Come quickly!"

They all came running. Christy waved her letter in the air triumphantly. "They're going to publish my story about Prince in the Asheville newspaper!"

"Christy, that's wonderful!" David cried, giving her a hug.

"I'm not the least bit surprised," Miss Alice said.

Christy passed the letter to Miss Alice. "See? The editor said my article will bring smiles of joy to his readers. And he's going to pay me, can you believe it? We can use the money for medicine, or maybe some books for the school."

"Miz Christy," Ruby Mae asked, "am I in the story?"

"Yes, you are, as a matter of fact. I talked about how you'd learned to be responsible and disciplined, caring for Prince."

"Me, in a big-city newspaper!" Ruby Mae said, shaking her head. "Imagine that!"

"The editor even asked if I had more stories about Cutter Gap that I wanted to send along," Christy said. "But I'll have to think about that."

Ruby Mae sighed heavily.

"What's wrong, Ruby Mae?" Miss Alice asked.

"Oh, nothin'. I was just a-wishin' Prince could be here to see all the fuss. He's goin' to be famous, and he won't even know it."

"I'm sure he'll hear about it, one way or another," David said with a tolerant smile.

"Maybe," Ruby Mae agreed. "I s'pose anything is possible."

"Miz Christy?" Ruby Mae asked that evening. "You mind some company?"

Christy was sitting in a rocker on the porch, a shawl around her shoulders. "Of course not. Come join me."

"Whatcha doin'?"

"Looking at the stars. And thinking."

"I been thinkin', too," Ruby Mae said. "Which I generally try not to do, what with it makin' my head hurt and all."

"What have you been thinking about, Ruby Mae? Maybe I can help you and your head won't hurt so much."

"Well, first off," Ruby Mae said, rocking back and forth in the chair next to Christy's, "I was thinkin' on how that big-city editor asked you to write more stories for him. Me, I got plenty o' stories about Cutter Gap folks saved up. I could help you out, if'n you got stuck."

"That's a very generous offer, Ruby Mae."

"And then, if you sold him a passel o' stories, you'd make a heap o' money, right?"

"Well, some, anyway."

Ruby Mae paused. "Probably enough so's you could buy Prince back from the mean folks at Great Oak Farm."

"How could we buy him back, Ruby Mae, when we don't even know where he is?"

Ruby Mae cast a nervous look at Christy. "Well, I *meant* s'posin' we found him—you know, way up in the woods somewheres. Then, when you got your money, we could buy him back, right?"

"Well, that presumes a lot. I'm not sure Mr. Collins would be interested in selling Prince."

"Oughta be. That Uriah man said he can't even ride him."

"I would certainly write those articles to help buy Prince back. But you can't buy a horse that isn't there. Besides, it would take a long time to earn enough money to buy Prince."

"Oh." Ruby Mae stopped rocking. She gazed up at the mountains, looming black shadows against a starlit sky. "How do you fight back, Miz Christy? I mean, when you ain't got nothin' to fight with? How do you beat a man like Mr. Collins?"

Christy sighed. "I don't know the answer to that question."

"But you're the teacher. You're *supposed* to know the answer."

"I do know this. It's something Miss Alice told me when I first came to these mountains and I was frightened by all the feuding and violence. She said that evil is real and powerful, and God is against evil all the way. She said we can try to persuade ourselves that evil doesn't exist, or keep quiet about it and say it's none of our business. Or we can work on God's side."

"But how? What if you don't know how?" Ruby Mae asked in a pleading voice.

More clearly than ever, Christy realized that if the children were hiding Prince, it wasn't just a game. They were protecting something they loved in the only way they knew how. Christy and David and Miss Alice knew it wouldn't last forever, that eventually Mr. Collins would track Prince down. But that didn't matter to Ruby Mae and her friends. What mattered to them was that they were fighting evil in the only way they could.

"Even a man like Mr. Collins has weaknesses," Christy said. "Perhaps, if he finds Prince and takes him back, he'll grow bored with him. Perhaps he'll get frustrated and embarrassed when Prince refuses to let him ride."

"Maybe."

"Sometimes even the most complicated story has a happy ending, Ruby Mae. You just have to have faith that with God's help we'll be able to change things."

"I'll try," Ruby Mae said softly. "One thing I *do* know how to do is pray."

Christy smiled. "I can't think of a better time to get in a little practice."

❧ Sixteen ❧

Miz Christy! It's Mr. Collins a-comin'," Ruby Mae called the next day. "And he's brung the sheriff with him!"

It was the noon break, and the children were spread out on the lawn outside the schoolhouse in small groups, eating their meager noon meal. Christy was sitting on the schoolhouse steps, grading the children's arithmetic tests from that morning.

She set the tests aside, watching as Jared Collins and three of his men approached on horseback. They pulled to a halt just inches from the steps.

"Afternoon, Miss Huddleston," Mr. Collins said, giving her a tip of his hat.

"Sheriff Bell, Mr. Collins, Mr. Wynne." Christy nodded curtly. "Is there something I can do for you?"

"Let's not play games, Miss Huddleston." Mr. Collins dismounted. "There are plenty of rumors floating around that Prince returned here. The only question is where you people are hiding him."

Christy cast a glance at the children, who were listening solemnly. "I honestly do not know where Prince is," she replied. "But if I did, I wouldn't want to return him to your men. Not after the way we saw him treated."

Mr. Collins tapped his riding crop in his palm, his dark eyes gleaming menacingly. "If you *did* know, then you would be in possession of stolen property. That's why I've brought along the sheriff today." Mr. Collins lowered his voice to a whisper that only Christy could hear. "And my guess is he'll pay a lot more attention to a wealthy landowner like me than to a poor mission worker like you."

Nearby, the children were murmuring amongst themselves. "I'm sorry I can't help you," Christy said firmly.

"I'd really hate to see anyone in this little backwater place have to go to jail," Mr. Collins continued. "What would these poor, unfortunate children do with their teacher locked up?" He clucked his tongue. "That would hardly be setting a good example, now, would it?" The sheriff, a lanky man with a serious air about him, cleared his throat.

"I'm afraid Mr. Collins here has a mighty good point, Miss Huddleston. I can't overlook the crime o' horse-stealin'. Around these parts that's a mighty serious offense." Christy gulped. Suddenly the gravity of what was happening hit her. But what could she do?

After a moment, Ruby Mae stepped forward. "S'posin'—now, I'm just s'posin', mind you—that a body did know where Prince was? Would there be any kind o' reward for his capture?"

Mr. Collins grinned. "Why, of course, young lady. How about . . . hmm . . . how about a nice gold coin for your trouble?"

"Truth to tell, I had somethin' else in mind."

Uriah nudged Mr. Collins. "*Told* ya they know where he is."

"I'm not sayin' I know, and I'm not sayin' I don't know," Ruby Mae said casually. "I'm just sayin' what if."

"What is it you'd like for a reward?" Mr. Collins asked. "Just name your price."

Ruby Mae smiled, just a little. "I want a competition."

"A—a competition? I'm afraid I don't know what you mean."

"I mean a fair-and-square, you-and-me competition."

Uriah laughed loudly. "How about it, Mr. C? Maybe you could arm-wrestle her!"

Mr. Collins was not amused. "You're wasting

my time," he snapped at Ruby Mae. "Two gold coins. That's my final offer."

"You and me, ridin' to see who gets Prince. If'n I wins, the mission gets to buy back Prince. May the best man—or gal—win," Ruby Mae responded. She crossed her arms over her chest and gave Mr. Collins her most determined look. "And that's *my* final offer."

"B—but—" Mr. Collins spluttered. He turned to Christy. "Can't you do something with this urchin? She's obviously in possession of my property. Tell her to hand over the horse, or I'll have her arrested."

"To begin with, Mr. Collins, I think that's exactly what Ruby Mae is proposing." Christy winked at Ruby Mae. "You know, Ruby Mae," she said, "if I didn't know better, I'd say this accomplished equestrian is afraid to compete against you."

"Yellow-belly," one of the older boys muttered.

Lundy made a noise like a squawking chicken, and soon the other children were chiming in until the schoolyard sounded more like a barnyard.

"That's enough, children," Christy said, trying to quiet her students.

"You wouldn't want to embarrass yourself in front of your own employees, now, would you, Mr. Collins?" Christy asked sweetly. "I'm sure you can beat Ruby Mae in a simple competition. What do you think, Ruby Mae? Three clean jumps over the fence in the pasture?"

"Bareback," Ruby Mae added.

Mr. Collins cleared his throat. "What on earth is the point in this? He's my horse, you fools!"

"Ain't no point in ownin' him, if'n you can't ride him," Ruby Mae pointed out.

"Aw, go ahead, Mr. C," Uriah said, with a wink at his fellow stable hands. "She's just a mite of a girl. If you can't handle that stallion, ain't no way she can."

Mr. Collins gazed at the sky and let out a frustrated groan. "Oh, all right. We'll let the country bumpkins have their fun." He shook his riding crop at Ruby Mae. "But we'll do it on my terms. You have the most clean jumps over that fence, little lady, I'll let you have the right to buy back Prince for the same money I paid for him. I'll give you three months to raise the cash. You lose, he's mine, and you never go near him again."

"Mr. Collins, we can't possibly raise that kind of money!" Christy protested.

Mr. Collins shrugged. "I'm giving you the chance to get your stallion back. Take my offer, or I'll have the sheriff arrest you."

"It's all right, Miz Christy," Ruby Mae said nervously. "It's the best we can do."

"At least give us this much," Christy pleaded.

"If Ruby Mae wins, we get three months to come up with the money. During that time, Prince stays here at the mission, not at your farm."

"Fine. Whatever," Mr. Collins said with a dismissive wave. "One way or another, he'll be mine, soon enough."

Ruby Mae held out her hand to Mr. Collins, and after a moment, he shook it. "Wait here. Lundy and me'll go get Prince. In the meantime, you might want to practice up. Oh, one other thing. When we get him back, we want Prince's bridle and his blanket back, too."

"I don't know what you're talking about," Mr. Collins snapped.

"I'll take care of that matter, Ruby Mae," Christy said.

Ruby Mae nodded. "Then it's settled."

Christy followed Ruby Mae to a spot out of Mr. Collins' earshot. "Are you sure you want to do this?" she asked.

"He was goin' to find him eventually," Ruby Mae said with a sigh. "It was just a matter of time. We all knew it."

"But even if you win, you have to understand that we won't have the money to buy Prince back, at least not right now."

"At least we'll have the *hope* o' buyin' him. That's somethin'. Thanks to you."

"To me?"

"For givin' me this idea. Last night, you

were talkin' about how even powerful people like Mr. Collins have their weaknesses. So I got to thinkin' what his were." She chuckled. "And I said to myself, 'I can ride Prince and he can't.' And that's how I come up with the idea."

"You do realize we'll have to come up with some kind of punishment for your horse-napping," Christy said with a tolerant smile.

Ruby Mae considered this for a moment. "You know what, Miz Christy?" she said. "Even if'n you punished me with a hundred spellin' tests, it'd be worth it, if it meant I got to protect Prince from gettin' hurt."

Lundy joined them. "Guess we'd best be gettin' on," he said.

"So where has Prince been all this time?" Christy asked.

"Over to Lundy's," Ruby Mae said. "Safe and sound."

"I guarded him best I could," Lundy said.

Christy patted Lundy on the back. "Prince is lucky to have such good friends."

"Don't speak too soon, Miz Christy," Ruby Mae warned. "This ain't over yet."

✺ Seventeen ✺

An hour later, everyone assembled in the pasture to watch the great competition unfold. Miss Alice, Miss Ida, and David were there, and so was Doctor MacNeill, who'd run into Lundy and Ruby Mae as they were bringing Prince back to the mission.

Prince seemed happy to see all his old friends, and to be the center of attention once again. But as soon as he caught sight of Mr. Collins, he tried to bolt.

"Whoa, boy," Ruby Mae said soothingly, clinging to the horse's bridle. "He ain't a-goin' to hurt you. Not while we're around to protect you."

"I told you that horse lacks manners," Mr. Collins said. "You can't handle him any better than I can."

"Just keep your distance," Ruby Mae snapped, "and I'll handle him just fine."

"All right," Christy announced, "it's time for the competition to begin. Each participant will attempt to make three clean jumps over that fence. The person with the most clean jumps wins."

"And no saddle, neither," Ruby Mae reminded her.

"All jumps will be bareback," Christy added. "Now, who would like to go first? Why don't we toss a coin? Doctor MacNeill, you may do the honors."

Doctor MacNeill retrieved a coin from his pocket. "Ruby Mae, call it when I toss the coin in the air."

"Heads!" Ruby Mae called as the coin spun around.

"Heads, it is," Doctor MacNeill reported.

"Then I'll go first," Ruby Mae said.

While David helped Ruby Mae mount Prince, Lundy swaggered over to Mr. Collins. "She'll show ya how it's done," he said, hooking his thumb at Ruby Mae. "Even if she is a girl, she's the finest rider around these parts."

"I doubt that's saying much," Mr. Collins sneered.

Ruby Mae gave Prince a gentle nudge with her knees, and he took off at an easy trot around the pasture. They moved together effortlessly. When she eased Prince into a full gallop, it was breathtaking to watch. Horse and rider glided over the grass, Prince's hooves thundering on the ground.

"Look at 'em go," Mountie said to Christy. "Ain't it just the purtiest thing to watch?"

Ruby Mae moved Prince around until he was facing the broken piece of four-foot-high fence that the children used for practicing jumps. They approached at a nice, steady pace, never wavering.

At just the right moment, Ruby Mae eased forward, holding tightly to Prince's mane. In one graceful move, Prince launched into the air like a huge bird. He and Ruby Mae sailed over the fence, and for a moment, the sound of his hooves fell silent, and the only noise was the gasp of the crowd.

He landed gently just past the mud hole on the other side of the fence. Ruby Mae turned to the crowd and gave a confident wave. Her classmates roared their approval.

"Well, I'll be," Uriah muttered. "That gal can ride, all right!"

"Shut up, Wynne," Mr. Collins snapped, "or you'll be looking for work."

Twice more, Ruby Mae took Prince over the fence. Twice more, the crowd broke into happy applause.

Ruby Mae reined Prince in to an easy trot, and brought him back to Mr. Collins. "See?"

she said. "Ain't nothin' to it." She slipped off Prince and passed the reins to Mr. Collins. "Now let's see what you can do."

"Perhaps—" Mr. Collins gazed up at the stallion nervously, "perhaps we should wait a few minutes. After all, he's probably quite winded."

"Naw." Ruby Mae shook her head. "Prince could jump a dozen o' those without breakin' a sweat. He's all nice and warmed up for you. Go on. I can't wait to see how a real, for-true e-ques-tri-an rides."

Eighteen

Mr. Collins grimaced. "I'll need a leg up. Uriah, come here. Cup your hands, and I'll use them instead of stirrups."

Uriah obliged, groaning under the weight. Prince danced around nervously, but Ruby Mae held him steady.

Awkwardly, Mr. Collins settled on Prince's back. Ruby Mae stepped aside. "Good luck to ya. Remember, take it nice and easy."

"I don't need your advice."

Mr. Collins dug his boot heels into Prince's sides. The stallion reared up in surprise. Mr. Collins clung to Prince's neck, and after a moment, the horse settled down.

This time, Mr. Collins cracked his riding crop on Prince's flank, sending the horse into a wild gallop.

"Whoa, Nellie," Ruby Mae said, letting out a

low whistle. "That sure is some funny-lookin' ridin'!"

Struggling to control Prince, Mr. Collins took him around the field twice in an all-out gallop. Finally, with great effort, he managed to face the stallion dead-on toward the fence.

"He's goin' too fast," Ruby Mae whispered to Christy, as Prince pounded toward the fence. "Look—Mr. Collins is losin' his grip. See how he's a-startin' to slip off?"

Suddenly, just as they reached the fence, Prince changed his mind about jumping. He careened to one side of the fence, coming to an abrupt halt.

Whoosh! Mr. Collins did *not* stop. He flew through the air, right over the fence, and landed with a plop directly in the mud puddle on the other side.

After a moment, he let out a low moan.

"Mr. C!" Uriah called. "You all right?"

Doctor MacNeill, Christy, and the others all ran to check on Mr. Collins.

"You'd better let me check for any broken bones," the doctor said, kneeling beside the mud-soaked Mr. Collins.

"Unhand me!" Mr. Collins shook off the doctor and slowly stood.

"My, oh my. Would you look at those purty ridin' clothes, all a-covered with mud?" Ruby Mae said, barely concealing her smile.

"The . . . the brute!" Mr. Collins shook his

riding crop at Prince, who was nibbling on some grass nearby, not aware of the trouble he'd caused.

"If that's how an e-ques-tri-an rides, I think I'll stick to my way o' doin' things," Ruby Mae continued.

"Um, sir," Uriah said under his breath, "ya got mud on yer nose."

Mr. Collins pulled out a handkerchief and wiped his face, which only managed to make things worse. Several of the children began giggling uncontrollably. Even Uriah laughed.

"That—that four-legged devil isn't worth a dollar!" Mr. Collins cried to Christy. "You and your pathetic tots can have him!"

"You mean he's ours again, for good?" Ruby Mae cried.

"We'll pay you what you paid us for Prince," Christy said. "It may take us more than three months, but you'll get your money back."

"Just promise me I'll never have to see his ugly face again," said Mr. Collins, his voice almost a shout.

With that, he stomped off across the pasture.

Ruby Mae turned to Christy and hugged her. She ran to Prince and hugged him. She even ran to Lundy and hugged him.

"He's ours! He's really, truly ours!" she cried.

"Hooray for Ruby Mae!" Mountie exclaimed,

and soon the entire group was chanting the same thing, over and over again.

Ruby Mae hopped onto Prince and took a victory lap around the pasture, followed by her classmates.

"So the story has a happy ending, after all," Miss Alice said to Christy as they watched the joyful children.

"As always, Miss Alice," Christy replied, "you were right."

"I think this might be a good time for a prayer of thanksgiving, don't you?" said Miss Alice, and Christy couldn't have agreed more.

~ ~ ~

The next day, another letter arrived for Christy. She opened it to discover a copy of her newspaper article, sent by her mother. "You're the talk of the town!" she'd written at the top of the page.

After school, Christy held a ceremony in Prince's honor outside the school. First, she read the article about him aloud.

The children were ecstatic about being "famous"—so much so that they didn't even mind the punishment Christy imposed for their horse-napping escapade. For one month, they had to muck out Prince's stall, and feed and water him every day.

Prince, however, was completely un-impressed with his new fame. In fact, he tried to eat the article.

"Now that we're done reading—and nib-bling—the article," Christy said, "I have one other thing I'd like to do. It's a presentation I've been meaning to make to Ruby Mae and Lundy."

Christy handed Lundy a wooden box. "Ruby Mae," she said, "why don't you open it?"

While Lundy held the box, Ruby Mae lifted the cover and gasped. "It's Prince's blanket! And his bridle! Miz Christy, how did you ever find them?"

"I've been saving them," Christy replied. "I had a feeling they might come in handy someday. That's one thing I've learned these past few weeks, children. Never, ever, give up hope."

About the Author

Catherine Marshall

With *Christy*, Catherine Marshall LeSourd (1914–1983) created one of the world's most widely read and best-loved classics. Published in 1967, the book spent 39 weeks on the New York Times bestseller list. With an estimated 30 million Americans having read it, *Christy* is now approaching its 90th printing and has sold more than eight million copies. Although a novel, *Christy* is in fact a thinly-veiled biography of Catherine's mother, Leonora Wood.

Catherine Marshall LeSourd also authored *A Man Called Peter*, which has sold more than four million copies. It is an American bestseller, portraying the love between a dynamic man and his God, and the tender, romantic love between a man and the girl he married.

Another one of Catherine's books is *Julie*, a powerful, sweeping novel of love and adventure, courage and commitment, tragedy and triumph, in a Pennsylvania town during the Great Depression. Catherine also authored many other devotional books of encouragement.

THE CHRISTY® FICTION SERIES

You'll want to read them all!

Based upon Catherine Marshall's international bestseller *Christy®*, this new series contains expanded adventures filled with romance, intrigue, and excitement.

#1—The Bridge to Cutter Gap
Nineteen-year-old Christy leaves her family to teach at a mission school in the Great Smoky Mountains. On the other side of an icy bridge lie excitement, adventure, and maybe even the man of her dreams . . . but can she survive a life-and-death struggle when she falls into the rushing waters below? (ISBN 0-8499-3686-1)

#2—Silent Superstitions
Christy's students are suddenly afraid to come to school. Is what Granny O'Teale says true? Is their teacher cursed? Will the children's fears and the adults' superstitions force Christy to abandon her dreams and return to North Carolina? (ISBN 0-8499-3687-X)

#3—The Angry Intruder
Someone wants Christy to leave Cutter Gap, and they'll stop at nothing. Mysterious pranks soon turn dangerous. Could a student be the culprit? When Christy confronts the late-night intruder, will it be a face she knows? (ISBN 0-8499-3688-8)

#4—Midnight Rescue
The mission's black stallion, Prince, has vanished, and so has Christy's student Ruby Mae. Christy must brave the guns of angry moonshiners to bring them home. Will her faith in God see her through her darkest night? (ISBN 0-8499-3689-6)

#5—The Proposal
Christy should be thrilled when David Grantland, the handsome minister, proposes marriage, but her feelings of excitement are mixed with confusion and uncertainty. Several untimely interruptions delay her answer to David's proposal. Then a terrible riding accident and blindness threaten all of Christy's dreams for the future. (ISBN 0-8499-3918-6)

#6—Christy's Choice
When Christy is offered a chance to teach in her hometown, she faces a difficult decision. Will her train ride back to Cutter Gap be a journey home or a last farewell? In a moment of terror and danger, Christy must decide where her future lies. (ISBN 0-8499-3919-4)

#7—The Princess Club
When Ruby Mae, Bessie, and Clara discover gold at Cutter Gap, they form an exclusive organization, "The Princess Club." Christy watches in dismay as her classroom—and her community—are torn apart by greed, envy, and an understanding of what true wealth really means. (ISBN 0-8499-3958-5)

#8—Family Secrets
Bob Allen and many of the residents of Cutter Gap are upset when a black family, the Washingtons, moves in near the Allens' property. When a series of threatening incidents befall the Washingtons, Christy steps in to help. But it's a clue in the Washingtons' family Bible that may hold the real key to peace and acceptance. (ISBN 0-8499-3959-3)

#9—Mountain Madness
When Christy travels alone to a nearby mountain, she vows to discover the truth behind the terrifying

legend of a strange mountain creature. But what she finds, at first seems worse than she ever imagined! (ISBN 0-8499-3960-7)

#10—Stage Fright

As Christy's students are preparing for a school play, she reveals her dream to act on stage herself. Little does she know that Doctor MacNeill's aunt is the artistic director of the Knoxville theater. Before long, just as Christy is about to debut on stage, several mysterious incidents threaten both her dreams and her pride! (ISBN 0-8499-3961-5)

#11—Goodbye, Sweet Prince

Prince, the mission's stallion, is sold to a cruel owner, then disappears. Christy Huddleston and her students are heartsick. Is there any way to reclaim the magnificent horse? (ISBN 0-8499-3962-3)

#12—Brotherly Love

Everyone is delighted when Christy's younger brother, George Huddleston, visits Christy at the Cutter Gap Mission. But the delight ends when George reveals that he has been expelled from school for stealing. Can Christy summon the love and faith to help her brother do the right thing? (ISBN 0-8499-3963-1)

Christy is now available on home videos through Broadman & Holman Publishers.